MR (NOT QUITE) PERFECT

BY
JESSICA HART

Published in Great Britain 2014
by Mills & Boon, an imprint of Harlequin (UK) Limited,
Eton House, 18-24 Paradise Road, Richmond, Surrey, TW9 1SR

© 2014 Jessica Hart

ISBN: 978 0 263 24156 3

Harlequin (UK) Limited's policy is to use papers that are natural,
renewable and recyclable products and made from wood grown in
sustainable forests. The logging and manufacturing processes conform
to the legal environmental regulations of the country of origin.

Printed and bound in Great Britain
by CPI Antony Rowe, Chippenham, Wiltshire

B000 0000108135

Jessica Hart was born in west Africa, and has suffered from itchy feet ever since, travelling and working around the world in a wide variety of interesting but very lowly jobs—all of which have provided inspiration on which to draw when it comes to the settings and plots of her stories. Now she lives a rather more settled existence in York, where she has been able to pursue her interest in history—although she still yearns sometimes for wider horizons.

If you'd like to know more about Jessica visit her website: www.jessicahart.co.uk

**This and other titles by Jessica Hart
are available in eBook format
from www.millsandboon.co.uk**

For John, perfect for me, with love.

CHAPTER ONE

MAKING MR PERFECT by Allegra Fielding

You've met a new guy. You're hot, hot, hot for each other. He's everything you ever wanted. But have you noticed that the infatuation phase never lasts? 'Fess up, ladies. How long before you're out with the girls and you find yourself saying, 'He'd be perfect if only he talked about his feelings/cooked occasionally/arranged a surprise mini-break/unfriended his ex on Facebook/insert peeve of your choice? He's still hot, you still love him to bits, but he's not quite as perfect as he seemed at first.

Are we asking too much of men nowadays? In a fairy tale, Prince Charming's task is clear. He has to hack his way through a thicket, slay a dragon and rescue the princess. Easy. In real life, we want our men to do a whole lot more to deserve us. Here at Glitz we've been conducting our own super-scientific survey over a few cocktails (pomegranate martinis, anyone?) and it seems that we want it all. The perfect boyfriend, it turns out, can fix our cars and dance without looking like a total dork. He looks good and he'll get rid of that spider in the shower. He'll sit through a romcom without complaining and be strong enough to literally sweep us off our feet when required.

But does such a man exist? And if he doesn't, is it possible to create him? Glitz gives one lucky guy the chance of the ultimate makeover. Read on and see how one unreconstructed male rose to the challenge of becoming the perfect man. Meet—

ALLEGRA LIFTED HER fingers from the keyboard and flexed them. Meet who?

Good question. Funny how the world was full of unreconstructed males until you actually needed one. But as soon as she had started asking around, it turned out that nobody wanted to admit that their boyfriends were anywhere near imperfect enough to take part in her experiment.

With a sigh, Allegra closed the document and shut down her computer. Had she been too ambitious? But Stella had liked the idea. The editor in chief had inclined her head by an infinitesimal degree, which signified enthusiasm. Now Allegra had a big break at last—and it would all fall apart if she couldn't find a man in need of a major makeover. One measly man, that was all she needed. He had to be out there somewhere…but where?

'Ouf!' Allegra threw herself extravagantly into the armchair and toed off her mock-croc stilettos with a grimace of pain. The needle-thin metal heels were to die for, but she had been on them for over twelve hours and while they might be long on style, they were extremely short on comfort.

Max didn't even look away from the television. He was stretched out on the sofa, flicking through channels, looking oddly at home in her sitting room. He had been tidying again, Allegra registered with a roll of her eyes. You would never catch the magazines being neatly lined up on the coffee table when it was just her and Libby. The radiators would be festooned with bras and thongs and the surfaces comfortingly cluttered with useful stuff like nail polish remover, empty shoe boxes, expired vouchers, cosmetic samples and screwed up receipts. She and Libby knew to check down the back of the sofa for chargers. They knew where they were with the mess.

There was no point in trying to tell Max that, though. Libby's brother was an engineer. They said cosy sitting room, he said tip.

She massaged her sore toes. 'My feet are *killing* me!'

'Why do you wear those ridiculous shoes?' Max demanded. 'It's like you put yourself through torture every day. Why don't you wear trainers or something more comfortable?'

'Because, Max, I work for *Glitz*,' said Allegra with exaggerated patience. 'That's a *fashion* magazine and, while I realise that as Mr Hasn't-got-a-clue you don't know what fashion is, I can assure you that my editor would send me home if I turned up in trainers!'

'They can't sack you for what you wear,' said Max, unimpressed.

'Stella can do whatever she likes.' Such was her editor's power and personality that Allegra found herself glancing over her shoulder and speaking in hushed tones whenever her name was mentioned.

'That woman's a monster. You should tell her where to get off.'

'And lose my job? Do you have any *idea* how hard it was to get a job at *Glitz*?' Cautiously Allegra wiggled the blood back into her poor toes. 'People kill for the chance to work with Stella. She's like the high priestess of fashion. She's totally awesome.'

'You're terrified of her.'

'I'm not terrified,' said Allegra, not quite honestly. 'I *respect* her. *Everyone* respects her.'

Everyone except her mother, of course, but then it took a lot to impress Flick Fielding, as Allegra knew to her cost. She suppressed a little sigh at the thought. She had been so hoping that Flick would approve of the fact that Stella had given her a job in the face of such competition, but her mother had only raised perfectly groomed brows.

'*Glitz?*' she'd echoed as if Allegra had boasted of a first journalist job with *Waste Collectors Weekly* instead of a top-selling glossy magazine. 'Well, if you're pleased, then of course…well done, darling.'

Allegra would never have applied to *Glitz* in the first place if she had known that Stella had once mocked Flick's choice of outfit for an awards ceremony. Flick, a formidably high-powered journalist, had not been amused.

Still, Allegra wouldn't allow herself to be downcast. She just needed to make her mark at *Glitz* and a good reference from Stella would make her CV stand out anywhere, whatever her mother might say. And *then* she would get a job that would really make Flick proud of her. Sadly, that would probably mean boning up on politics and economics rather than shoes and handbags, but she would worry about that when the time came. For now the important thing was to impress Stella.

'Well, I think you're mad,' said Max. 'It's bad enough having to wear a suit to work every day.'

Allegra eyed the striped polo shirt that Max changed into the moment he got home with disfavour. 'Thank God they *do* make you wear a suit,' she said. 'Even you can't go too far wrong with a suit and tie. The rest of the time, it's like you've got an unerring sense of what will be *least* stylish.'

'What do you mean?'

'Well, take that…*that*,' she said, pointing at his top and Max looked down at his chest.

'What's wrong with it?'

'It's hideous!'

'It's comfortable,' he said, unbothered. 'I don't care about style.'

'You don't say,' said Allegra sarcastically.

It was quite incredible how lively Libby had ended up with such a stuffy brother! Max didn't have a clue about music, or clothes, or anything other than engineering, as far as Allegra could tell. He didn't look *too* bad in a conventional suit, but his taste in casual wear made her wince every time.

'I wouldn't even use that thing you're wearing as a duster,' she said.

'You wouldn't use anything as a duster,' Max countered. 'You never do any housework.'

'I do!'

'Where does the dustpan and brush live?'

There was a pause. 'Under the sink?'

He made a bleeping noise. 'In the cupboard under the stairs.'

'There's a cupboard under the stairs?'

'I rest my case.' Max shook his head and returned his attention to the television.

Gingerly, Allegra tested her feet and decided that she could manage a hobble to the kitchen to find something to eat. She was starving. Like the sitting room, the kitchen was so tidy nowadays she hardly recognized it.

Max had moved in a couple of weeks earlier. Libby's three-month placement in Paris had coincided with the break-up of her brother's engagement, and she had offered him her room while she was away.

'Would you mind?' she had asked Allegra. 'It's only for a couple of months before he'll get a chance to go out to Shofrar, so it's hard for him to find somewhere temporary. And I'm worried about him. You know what Max is like; he's not exactly big on talking about feelings, but I think he must be really gutted about Emma.'

'Why did she break it off, do you know?' Allegra had been shocked when she heard. She'd only met Emma a couple of times, but she'd seemed perfect for Max. An engineer like him, Emma had been pretty, nice...the word *boring* shimmered in Allegra's head but it was too unkind so she pushed it away...practical, she decided instead. Exactly the kind of sensible girl Max would choose and the last person Allegra would have expected to have broken it all off six months before the wedding.

'He hasn't told me.' Libby shook her head. 'Just says it's all for the best. But I know he was planning for them to go out to Shofrar together and now that's all off...well, I'd feel better if you were around to cheer him up. As long as you really don't mind.'

'Of course I don't mind,' said Allegra. She'd been at school with Libby and had spent many holidays with her friend's family while Flick was working. Max was the brother she had never had, and over the years she had bickered with him and relied on him almost as much as Libby did.

'At least I know he's not a serial killer or anything,' she'd said cheerfully. 'I'll stop him missing Emma too much.'

In fact, she didn't see much of him. Max left for work early in the morning, and she was out most evenings. When they did coincide, like now, Max grumbled about her untidiness and Allegra criticised his clothes. They fought over the remote and shared the occasional take-away. It was all perfectly comfortable.

And why wouldn't it be? Allegra asked herself as she opened the fridge and studied its contents without enthusiasm. This was Max, after all. Libby's brother. Allegra was fond of him, when she wasn't being irritated by his wardrobe and that way he had of making her feel like an idiot a lot of the time. Max wasn't ugly, but he wasn't exactly a hunk either. Certainly not a man to set your heart pattering.

Apart from that one night, of course. Don't forget that.

Allegra sighed as she picked out a low-fat yoghurt. Did everyone have an irritating voice in their head that would pop up at the least convenient times to remind them of precisely the things they most wanted to forget?

And it wasn't a night, she felt compelled to argue with herself, rummaging for a teaspoon. It had been an odd little incident, that was all. Not even an incident, really. *A moment.* And so long ago, really she had almost forgotten it.

Or she would have done if that pesky voice would let her.

No, it was all very comfortable. It was *fine.* Allegra was glad Max wasn't gorgeous or sexy. It made it easy to be relaxed with him. Which wasn't to say he couldn't make more of an effort on the clothes front. He didn't seem to care what he looked like, Allegra thought critically. That shirt was appalling and he *would* fasten it almost to the neck, no matter how often she told him to undo another button. He had no idea at all. If he smartened himself up a bit…

And that was when it hit her. Allegra froze with the teaspoon in her mouth.

Max. He was *perfect!* Why on earth hadn't she thought of him before?

She'd pitched the 'create a perfect boyfriend' idea to Stella at an editorial meeting the previous week. It was the first of her ideas that she'd been given the go-ahead to follow up, and Allegra had been fired with enthusiasm at first. But she had begun to wonder if she could make it work without the right man.

And now she had found him, lying in her own sitting room!

Already Allegra's mind was leaping forward, all her excitement about the project refuelled. She would write the best article *ever*. It would be fun, it would be interesting, it would tap into every woman's fantasy of making her man perfect. It would win awards, be syndicated worldwide. Stella would gasp with admiration.

At this point Allegra's imagination, vivid as it was, faltered. Stella, gasping? But a little strategic tweaking and the fantasy still worked. All right, Stella would look as enigmatic as ever but her words would be sweet. *Allegra*, she would say, *you're our new star writer. Have a massive salary.*

I'd love to, Stella, Allegra imagined herself saying in reply, super casual. *But the* Financial Times *has made me an offer I can't refuse.*

Surely her mother would be impressed by the *FT*?

Sucking yoghurt thoughtfully from her spoon, Allegra went to the kitchen doorway from where she could study Max without being observed.

He was still on the sofa, still flicking through channels in search of the news or sport, which was all he ever watched. Definitely not the kind of guy you would check out in a bar. Brown hair, ordinary features, steady blue-grey eyes: there was nothing wrong with him, but nothing special either.

Yep, he was perfect.

Max played rugby so he was pretty fit, but he didn't make anything of himself. Allegra mentally trimmed his hair and got rid of the polo shirt only to stop, unnerved, when she realised that the image of him lying on the sofa bare-chested was quite…startling.

Hastily, she put the shirt back on in her imagination. Whatever, the man was ripe for a makeover.

All she had to do was get Max to agree. Scraping out the yoghurt pot, Allegra tossed it in the bin with a clatter and squared her shoulders. Only last week she'd written an article on the benefits of thinking positive and getting what you wanted. It was time to put all that useful research into practice.

Back in the sitting room, she batted at Max's knees until he shifted his legs and she could plonk herself down on the sofa next to him. 'Max,' she began carefully.

'No.' Max settled his legs back across her lap and crossed his ankles on the arm of the sofa, all without taking his eyes off the television.

'What do you mean, *no*?' Forgetting her determination to stay cool and focused, as per her own advice in the article, Allegra scowled at him. 'You don't know what I'm going to say yet!'

'I know that wheedling tone of old,' said Max. 'You only use it when you want me to do something I'm not going to want to do.'

'Like what?' she said, affronted.

'Like waste an entire hot bank holiday Monday sitting in traffic because you and Libby wanted to go to the sea.'

'That was Libby's idea, not mine.'

'Same wheedle,' said Max, still flicking channels. 'And it was definitely your idea to have a New Year's Eve party that time.'

'It was a great party.'

'And who had to help you clear up afterwards before my parents came home?'

'You did, because you're a really, really kind brother who likes to help his sister and his sister's best mate out when they get into trouble.'

Max lowered the remote and looked at Allegra in alarm.

'Uh-oh. You're being nice. That's a bad sign.'

'How can you say that? I'm often nice to you. Didn't I make you a delicious curry last weekend?'

'Only because you wanted some and didn't want to admit that you'd broken your diet.'

Sadly, too true.

'*And* I said I'd go to that dinner and pretend to be your fiancée,' she said. 'How much nicer can I get?'

Max pulled himself up to look at Allegra with suddenly narrowed eyes. 'You're not going to back out, are you? Is that what this is about? Now that Emma's not around, I really need you.'

'Aw, Max, that's sweet!'

'I'm serious, Legs. My career depends on this.'

'I do think the whole thing is mad.' Allegra wriggled into a more comfortable position, not entirely sorry to let the conversation drift while she worked out exactly how to persuade Max to agree to take part. 'I mean, who cares nowadays if you're married or not?'

'Bob Laskovski does,' said Max gloomily.

At first he had welcomed the news that the specialist firm of consulting engineers he worked for was to be taken over by a large American company. An injection of capital, jobs secured, a new CEO with fantastic contacts with the Sultan of Shofrar and some major projects being developed there and elsewhere in the Middle East: it was all good news.

The bad news was that the new CEO in question was

a nut. Bob Laskovski allegedly had a bee in his bonnet about the steadying influence of women, of all things. If ever there was going to be unsettling going on, there was bound to be a female involved, in Max's opinion. But Bob liked his project managers to be in settled relationships and, given the strict laws of Shofrar, that effectively meant that, male or female, they had to be married.

'God knows what he thinks we'll do if we don't have a wife to come home to every night,' Max had grumbled to Allegra. 'Run amok and seduce local girls and offend the local customs, I suppose.'

Allegra had just laughed. 'I'd love to see you running amok,' she'd said.

Max had ignored that and ploughed on with his explanation. 'If I don't turn up with a likely-looking fiancée, Bob's going to start humming and hawing about whether I'm suitable for the job or not.'

It was ridiculous, he grumbled whenever given the opportunity. He had the skills, he had the experience, and he was unencumbered by ties. He should be the perfect candidate.

There hadn't been a problem when Bob had first said that he was coming over to London and wanted to meet the prospective project managers. That was another of Bob's 'things', apparently: he liked to vet them personally over individual dinners. God knew how the man had had the time to build up a vast construction company.

Max hadn't thought about it too much when the invitation to dinner had arrived. He and Emma had been going to get married anyway, and she was bound to go down well with Bob. Max was all set for his big break.

And then Emma had changed her mind.

Max still couldn't quite believe it. He might have lost his fiancée, but he was damned if he was going to lose the

Shofrar job too. Still, at least Allegra had been quite willing to help when he broached the idea of her standing in for Emma. For all her silliness, she could be counted on when it mattered.

'But just for an evening,' she had warned. 'I'm not going to marry you and go out to Shofrar just so you can be a project manager!'

'Don't worry, it won't come to that,' said Max, shuddering at the very thought of it.

'There are plenty of examples of relationships busting up before and after engineers get out there, and once you're actually doing the job and behaving yourself it's not a problem. All I need to do is get Bob's seal of approval. Everyone says it's worth humouring him.

'It'll just be a dinner,' he assured her. 'All you need to do is smile and look pretty and pretend that you're going to be the perfect engineer's wife.'

Of course, *that* was going to be the problem. He'd eyed Allegra critically. She'd been dressed in a short stretchy skirt that showed off her long legs, made even longer by precarious heels. 'Maybe you'd better wear something a bit more…practical,' he'd said. 'You don't really look like an engineer's wife.'

Allegra, of course, had taken that as a compliment.

'I don't mind going along to the dinner with you,' she said now. 'I may not be much of an actress, but I expect I can pretend to love you for an evening.'

'Thanks, Legs,' said Max. 'It means a lot to me.'

'But…' she said, drawing out the word, and his eyes narrowed suspiciously; he never liked the sound of 'but'. '…there *is* just one tiny thing you could do for me in return.'

She smiled innocently at him and his wary look deepened. 'What?'

'No, your line is, *Of course, Allegra, I'll do whatever you want.* Would you like to try it again?'

'What?' he repeated.

Allegra sighed and squirmed round until she was facing him. She tucked her hair behind her ears, the way she did when she was trying to look serious, and fixed him with her big green eyes.

'You know how hard it's been for me to make my mark at *Glitz*?'

Max did. He knew more than he wanted, in fact, about Allegra's precarious foothold on the very lowest rung of the glossy magazine, where as far as he could make out, emotions ran at fever-pitch every day and huge dramas erupted over shoes or handbags or misplaced emery boards. Or something equally pointless.

Allegra seemed to love it. She raced into the flat, all long legs and cheekbones and swingy, shiny hair, discarding scarves and shoes and earrings as she went, and whirled out again in an outfit that looked exactly the same, to Max's untutored eye.

She was always complaining, though, that no one at the magazine noticed her. Max thought that was extremely unlikely. Allegra might not be classically beautiful but she had a vivid face with dark hair, striking green eyes and a mobile expression. She wasn't the kind of girl people didn't notice.

He'd known her since Libby had first brought her home for the holidays. Max, callous like most boys his age, had dismissed her at first as neurotic, clumsy and overweight. For a long time she'd just been Libby's gawky friend, but she'd shed the weight one summer and, while it was too much to say that she'd emerged a butterfly from her chrysalis, she had certainly gained confidence. Now she was really quite attractive, Max thought, his gaze resting on her face and drifting, quite without him realising, to her mouth.

He jerked his eyes away. The last time he'd found himself looking at her mouth, it had nearly ended in disaster. It had been before he'd met Emma, a moment of madness one night when all at once things seemed to have changed. Max still didn't know what had happened. One moment he and Allegra had been talking, and the next he'd been staring into her eyes, feeling as if he were teetering on the edge of a chasm. Scrabbling back, he'd dropped his gaze to her mouth instead, and that had been even worse.

He'd nearly kissed Allegra.

How weird would *that* have been? Luckily they'd both managed to look away at last, and they'd never referred to what had happened—or not happened—ever again. Max put it out of his mind. It was just one of those inexplicable moments that were best not analysed, and it was only occasionally, like now, when the memory hurtled back and caught him unawares, a sly punch under his ribs that interfered oddly with his breathing.

Max forced his mind back to Allegra's question. 'So what's changed?' he asked her, and she drew a deep breath.

'I've got my big break! I've got my own assignment.'

'Well, great...good for you, Legs. What's it going to be? A hard-hitting exposé of corruption in the world of shoes? Earth-shattering revelations on where the hemline is going to be next year?'

'Like I'd need your help if it was either of those!' said Allegra tartly. 'The man who wouldn't know fashion if it tied him up and slapped him around the face with a wet fish.'

'So what do you need me for?'

'Promise you'll hear me out before you say anything?'

Max swung his legs down and sat up as he eyed Allegra

with foreboding. 'Uh-oh, I'm starting to get a bad feeling about this!'

'*Please*, Max! Just listen!'

'Oh, all right,' he grumbled, sitting back and folding his arms. 'But this had better be good.'

'Well…' Allegra moistened her lips. 'You know we have an editorial conference to plan features for the coming months?'

Max didn't, but he nodded anyway. The less he had to hear about the workings of *Glitz*, the better.

'So the other day we were talking about one of the girls whose relationship has just fallen apart.'

'This is *work*? Gossiping about relationships?' It didn't sound like any conference Max had ever been in.

'Our readers are *interested* in relationships.' Allegra's straight, shiny hair had swung forward again. She flicked it back over her shoulder and fixed him with a stern eye. 'You're supposed to be just listening,' she reminded him.

'So, yes, we were talking about that and how her problem was that she had totally unrealistic expectations,' she went on when Max subsided with a sigh. 'She wanted some kind of fairy tale prince.'

Princes. Fairy tales. Max shook his head. He thought about his own discussions at work: about environmental impact assessments and deliverables and bedrock depths. Sometimes it seemed to him that Allegra lived in a completely different world.

'We had a long discussion about what women really want,' she went on, ignoring him. 'And we came to the conclusion that actually we want everything. We want a man who can fix a washing machine and plan the perfect date. Who'll fight his way through a thicket if required but who can also dress well and talk intelligently at the theatre. Who can plan the perfect romantic date and sort out your tax and dance and communicate...'

Max had been listening with growing incredulity. 'Good luck finding a bloke who can do all that!'

'Exactly!' Allegra leant forward eagerly. '*Exactly*! That was what we all said. There isn't anyone like that out there. So I started thinking: what if we could *make* a man like that? What if we could create a boyfriend who was everything women wanted?'

'How on earth would you go about that?' asked Max, not sure whether to laugh or groan in disbelief.

'By teaching him what to do,' said Allegra. 'That's what I pitched to Stella: a piece on whether it's possible to take an ordinary bloke and transform him into the perfect man.'

There was a silence. Max's sense of foreboding was screaming a warning now.

'Please tell me this isn't the point where you say, *And this is where you come in*,' he said in a hollow voice.

'And this is where you come in, Max,' said Allegra.

He stared at her incredulously. She was smiling, and he hoped to God it was because she was winding him up. 'You're not serious?'

'Think about it: you're the ideal candidate. You haven't got a girlfriend at the moment...and frankly,' she added, unable to resist, 'unless you get rid of that polo shirt, you won't get another one.'

Max scowled. 'Stop going on about my shirt. Emma never minded it.'

'Maybe she never *said* she minded it, but I bet she did.' On a roll, Allegra pointed a finger at Max. 'The thing is, Max, that shirt is symptomatic of a man who can't be bothered to make an effort. I'm guessing Emma was just too nice to point that out.'

Max ground his teeth. 'For God's sake, Allegra! It's

comfortable. Since when has comfort been an indictable offence?'

'There are plenty of other new comfortable shirts out there that aren't striped or buttoned too high at the collar, but you won't buy them because that would mean changing, and changing is hard work,' said Allegra. 'And it's not just a question of clothes. You need to change how you communicate, how you *are*. How much effort you put into thinking about your girlfriend and what will make her happy.'

Closing his eyes briefly, Max drew a breath and let it out with exaggerated patience. 'Allegra, I have no idea what you're talking about,' he said.

'Why did Emma call off your engagement? I'll bet it was because you weren't prepared to make an effort, wasn't it?'

'No, it wasn't,' said Max, goaded at last. 'If you must know, she met someone else. It's not as if it's a big secret,' he went on, seeing Allegra's awkward expression. It was obviously just as much a surprise to her as it had been to him. 'I just don't particularly feel like talking about it all the time.'

'Emma seemed so nice,' said Allegra hesitantly after a moment. 'She didn't seem like someone who'd cheat on you.'

'She didn't.' Max blew out a breath, remembering how unprepared he had been for Emma's revelation. 'She was very honest. She said she'd met someone who works for one of our clients, and she didn't want to sleep with him until she'd told me how he made her feel. He made her realise that we didn't have any passion in our relationship any more.'

'Eeuww.'

That was exactly what Max had thought. 'I mean,

passion!' He practically spat out the word. 'What in God's name does *passion* mean?'

'Well, I suppose…sexual chemistry,' Allegra offered. She hesitated. 'So were things in the bedroom department…?' She trailed off delicately.

'They were fine! Or I thought they were fine,' Max amended bitterly. 'I loved Emma, and I thought she loved me. She was always talking about how compatible we were. We had the same interests. We were *friends*. It was her idea to get married in the first place, and I couldn't see any reason not to. We'd been together three years and it was the obvious next step.

'Then Emma meets this guy and suddenly it's all about magic and chemistry and getting swept off her feet!' Max's mouth twisted. 'I said to her, magic doesn't last. Having things in common is more important than sparks, but she wouldn't listen to reason.' He sighed, remembering. 'It was so unlike her. Emma used to be so sensible. It was one of the things I loved about her. She wasn't silly like—'

Like you.

Max managed to bite the words back in time, but he might as well not have bothered because they hung in the air anyway.

Allegra told herself she didn't mind. She had more important things to worry about, like getting her assignment off the ground.

'I don't think you should give up on Emma, Max,' she said persuasively. 'You two were good together. It sounds to me as if she was feeling taken for granted.'

'You being the great relationship expert,' said Max dourly.

'I know what I'm talking about when it comes to failed relationships,' Allegra pointed out, unfazed. 'It wouldn't surprise me at all if Emma is just looking for more attention from you. And that's where I can help you,' she added cunningly, gaining confidence from the fact that Max hadn't scoffed yet. 'If you really want her back, put yourself in my hands. It's a win for all of us, Max. I get my article written, you get Emma back, and Emma gets the perfect man!'

CHAPTER TWO

THERE WAS A long silence. Max's eyes were narrowed. He was definitely thinking about it, Allegra realised jubilantly, and she forced herself not to say any more. If he felt she was pressurising him, he would back away. Softly, softly, catchee monkey.

'What *exactly* would be involved?' he asked cautiously at last, and Allegra kept her eyes downcast so that he wouldn't see the triumph in them. She didn't want to spook him now.

'The idea is for you to complete a series of tasks,' she began. 'Sort of like a knightly quest…' She stopped as his face changed. Oops, looked like she'd lost him already with the knightly quest. Hurriedly, Allegra switched tactics. Practical details, that would appeal to Max.

'So your first task would be to have cocktails—'

'I can't stand those poncy drinks,' he started grumbling immediately. 'I don't know how you women can sit there sucking through straws and fighting your way through umbrellas and cherries.'

'—with Darcy King,' Allegra finished talking over the top of him.

A pause. Max sat up straight. 'What, not…?'

'Yes, *the* Darcy King.'

Idiot. She should have mentioned Darcy right at the

start. Darcy was every red-blooded male's fantasy, a lingerie model with a sweet face and a sinful body. Allegra could practically see Max drooling already. If Darcy wouldn't win him round to the assignment, nothing would.

'You, Max Warriner, have the chance to go on a series of dates with Darcy King herself. Think about what your mates will say when they hear about *that!*'

'Darcy King wouldn't want to go out with me!'

'Not if you were wearing that shirt, she wouldn't, but that's the whole point,' said Allegra at her most persuasive. 'Can we take you—an engineer with no dress sense and rudimentary social skills but with some useful abilities like how to put a flat pack from Ikea together—and turn you into the sophisticated, well-dressed kind of man that Darcy would like to go out with?'

Max looked as if he wasn't sure how to take that. 'She must have a boyfriend already, looking like that.'

'Apparently she finds it hard to find men who can get past what she looks like and be interested in *her*,' said Allegra. 'Ianthe interviewed her a couple of months ago and it turns out she's just like the rest of us, kissing a lot of toads and still hoping to find her prince.'

On the other side of the sofa, Max didn't bother to disguise his incredulity. 'And you think *I* could be Darcy King's prince?'

'Actually, no.' Hmm, this was tricky. She didn't want to discourage him, but it wouldn't be fair to get his hopes up either. 'I mean, even if you were to fall madly in love, it's hard to imagine you having a future together. I don't see Darcy wanting to go off to Shofrar.'

'True. There's not a lot of work for lingerie models out there,' Max agreed. 'But if we were madly in love, would that matter?'

For one awful moment Allegra thought that he was

taking the whole matter seriously, but when she shot him a worried look he didn't quite have time to conceal the mocking gleam in his blue-grey eyes, and she grinned and shoved him.

'You know what I mean,' she said. 'It's just a fun assignment, but Darcy gets to have a good time, and you might learn something about dealing with women. If you want to get Emma back, Max, this could be just the chance you need. Are you really going to turn it down because you don't want to be seen sucking a cocktail through a straw?'

Max considered her. 'That would be it? Drinking a cocktail with Darcy King?'

'Well, obviously we'd need to make a few changes,' said Allegra airily. 'Get you a new wardrobe, a new haircut, that kind of thing, but the stylist would help you with that.'

'*Stylist?*'

'You're really lucky.' Allegra lowered her voice reverentially. 'Dickie said he'd style the shoot personally.'

'Shoot? What shoot? And who the hell is Dickie?'

He really didn't have a clue, did he? 'Dickie Roland is only the most famous stylist in London at the moment,' she said. 'He's a superstar! I think his name is actually Georges, but in the fashion world he's just known as Dickie after his trademark bow tie. He's worn it ever since he came to London from Paris, and it's hard to imagine him without one now.'

'I hope you're not planning to ask me to wear a bow tie!'

'No, no, that's Dickie's "thing". He'll just make you look fabulous.' Allegra sighed. Max clearly had no idea what an honour it was to be styled by Dickie. 'But you have to promise to be nice to him. Dickie's brilliant, but he can be a bit…temperamental.'

Max pinched the bridge of his nose. 'I can't believe I'm actually discussing being styled!' he muttered.

'You'd want to look nice for Darcy, wouldn't you?'

'I haven't said yes yet,' he warned quickly. 'What else is involved in this assignment of yours? It's got to be more than putting on a shirt and slurping a cocktail.'

'Once you've got through the cocktails, the next task is to cook Darcy dinner—and no ordering in a pizza. You have to cook it yourself.' Darcy was a vegetarian and the meal had to be a romantic one, but Allegra would break that to Max later. For now she just had to get him to agree in principle. There would be time enough to talk him through the pesky details once he'd agreed.

Max grunted. 'I could probably manage a meal, as long as she's not expecting anything fancy.'

'The whole point is to make an effort to cook something *Darcy* would like,' said Allegra, smoothing impatience from her voice. It wouldn't do to put his back up now, just when she had him nibbling at her hook! 'When you're having a drink, you'll have to talk to her and find out what sort of food she prefers, and if she likes fancy, then you're going to have to cook fancy. But I wouldn't be surprised if she likes things simple,' she added hastily as Max's brows drew together.

'Okay. So cocktail, cooking...what else?'

Best to take the next bit in a rush. 'You'd need to do something cultural without looking bored—we're thinking the theatre, perhaps, or the opening of an art exhibition—and that's it, really. Then it's just the ball,' Allegra finished breezily and put on a bright smile, hoping that Max might have missed the last task.

No such luck. 'Please tell me you're thinking about a round thing that you kick around a field!'

'Not *exactly*...'

'Come on, Legs, there's something you're not telling me, isn't there?'

'All right, it's a costume ball being held for charity. You'll have to dress up—and learn to waltz.'

There, it was out, but, as expected, Max had started shaking his head at 'costume'. 'No way,' he said firmly. 'I don't mind having a go at the other stuff, but dressing up? And *dancing?* I'd rather stick pins in my eyes!'

'Oh, Max, *please!* We have to have the ball. Darcy's really looking forward to it, and learning how to dance would be such a great gesture. It would be so…*romantic.*'

'What's romantic about making a tit of yourself on the dance floor?'

'I've always wanted to go to a ball like that. Not just a dinner dance bash but a real ball, with proper ball gowns and waltzing…' Allegra's eyes were dreamy at the mere thought of it, and she pressed a hand to the base of her throat as she sighed.

She had grown up in a house full of books, but Flick's shelves were lined with heavyweight biographies and award-winning literary novels. Flick was dismissive of commercial fiction, and as a child Allegra's books had been uniformly worthy. It had been a revelation to go and stay with Libby's family, where the house was full of dog-eared paperbacks with broken spines and yellowing pages.

Best of all, Max's mother had a collection of Regency romances and Allegra had devoured them every time she went. She loved the ordered world they portrayed with those rakish dukes and spirited governesses. She loved the dashing way the heroes drove their curricles, their curling lips, their codes of honour.

And their tight breeches, of course.

Best of all were the ball scenes, which were charged with sexual tension as the hero and heroine clasped hands and danced, oblivious to anyone but each other.

A wistful sigh leaked out of her. 'I'd love to waltz,' she

told Max, who was predictably unimpressed. 'It's my fantasy to be swept masterfully around a ballroom by a dashing hero, who knows just how to dance me unobtrusively out onto a terrace where it's dark and warm and the air is sweet with the scent of summer flowers and he's dancing with me along the terrace but he's overcome by passion and he presses me up against the balustrade and tells me he loves me madly and can't live without me and he's begging me to marry him—'

Running out of breath, she broke off to find Max watching her quizzically.

'I'm glad you stopped,' he said. 'I was wondering if I should throw a glass of water at you to stop you hyperventilating.'

'You've got to admit it would be romantic,' Allegra insisted.

Max showed no sign of admitting any such thing. He got back to the business in hand.

'Why not get that boyfriend of yours to take you if you want to go so much? What's his name? Jerry?'

'Jeremy.'

'That's right. Of course he's a Jeremy,' said Max dismissively. 'I bet he knows how to dance. I only met him once but he struck me as a guy who knows how to do everything.'

Jeremy had been very accomplished, that was for sure, but he was much too serious to go dancing. He was interested in politics and the economy. He could talk about the arts and international relations. He had been well-dressed and charming. Not the most practical guy in the world perhaps, but Allegra couldn't imagine him ever needing to assemble any flat packs in any case.

'In fact, why not get him to do your whole assignment?'

Max said and Allegra sighed and tucked her legs more comfortably beneath her.

'It wouldn't be much of a transformation story,' she said. 'Besides, I haven't seen him for a while. He wasn't really my boyfriend.'

She had tried to be upset when Jeremy stopped calling, but honestly, it had been a relief not to have to try quite so hard for a while. Jeremy's conversation might be impressive but it was light on humour and, in spite of growing up with Flick Fielding as a mother, the sad truth was that Allegra's interests veered more towards celebrity gossip and shoes than political intrigue. Flick would be appalled if she had guessed, and Allegra did her best not to disappoint her mother, but sometimes it was hard to keep up.

'We only went out a couple of times,' she said. 'Jeremy was just…someone Flick introduced me to.'

That would be right, thought Max. Allegra's mother liked to keep her daughter toeing the line and would soon veto any unsuitable boyfriends. Tricky Flicky, as she was known by those unfortunate enough to have been subjected to one of her gruelling interviews, was a media heavyweight, famous as much for her style as for her incisive questioning. Much as they might squirm under the lash of her tongue and steely-eyed gaze, politicians lobbied to be interviewed by Flick Fielding. Flick had gravitas, they all agreed that.

Whereas Allegra…Allegra was warm and funny and creative and kind, but gravitas? No.

Max had never understood why Flick, with all her brains, didn't just accept that rather than trying to force Allegra into her own mould.

'So, you're not heartbroken?' he asked Allegra cautiously. Because he had learnt that with women you never could tell.

'No.' Allegra blew out a long sigh and pushed her hair away from her face. 'Jeremy was just the latest in a long line of men who turned out not to be The One after all. I had such high hopes when I first met him too.'

'You know, you might get on better if you stopped letting your mother choose your boyfriends.' Max kept his voice carefully neutral but Allegra bridled anyway.

'She doesn't *choose* them!'

'Come on, when have you ever gone out with someone your mother wouldn't approve of?'

'I happen to like men who are attractive and intelligent and witty and successful,' Allegra said defensively. 'Of course she approves of them.'

'Maybe I should have said that you should try going out with someone because you like him, not because you think your mother will.'

'I *did* like Jeremy.' Clearly ruffled, Allegra wriggled her shoulders. 'Anyway, that's all beside the point. Jeremy's not around and you are, and Max, you're *perfect* for my assignment! There's so much scope for you to improve.'

'Thanks a lot!'

'You know what I mean. You could get so much out of it too. You should be leaping at the chance to learn how to give a woman what she really wants! You're going to Shofrar in a couple of months and the piece won't be out until after you leave, but if you play your cards right you could win Emma back and take her with you. That's what you want, isn't it?'

Was it? Max thought about Emma. She'd been so easy to be with. They'd been comfortable together, and it would be good to have that back again. Of course he wanted her back…but he wanted her the way she had been before she lost her head and started wanting more of everything: more excitement, more passion, more attention, more effort. Max thought the whole idea was to find someone you didn't *have* to make an effort for, but apparently he was wrong about that.

He missed Emma, though, and he missed the warm feeling of knowing that you'd found the woman you wanted to settle down with. He would never find anyone better than Emma. She was perfect for him.

'Yes,' he said. 'Of course I do.'

'Well, then,' said Allegra, satisfied. 'I bet if Emma gets wind of the fact that you're going out with Darcy she'll be jealous.'

'I wouldn't really be going out with her,' Max pointed out.

'Emma won't know that, will she? She'll be back in no time, you'll see.'

'I don't know.' Max pulled down his mouth. 'I wouldn't bet on it, and in the meantime I really don't want to dress up and learn to dance just on the off chance that she does. I can't imagine Emma caring about whether I can waltz or not.'

'You couldn't imagine her being carried away by passion either,' Allegra pointed out.

'No, but—'

It was at that point that Allegra gave up on arguments and threw pride to the winds. Grabbing his hand, she held it between her own.

'Oh, please, Max! Please, please, please, please, *please!* Please say you'll do it! This is my big chance to impress Stella. If I don't find someone to take part in this assignment, I won't get another one. I'll be a failure!' she said extravagantly. 'My career will be over before it's begun and how will I tell Flick?'

She leant beseechingly towards him and Max found himself snared in the big eyes. Funny how he had never noticed before how beautiful they were, or how green, the lovely dark mossy green of a secret wood…

Secret wood? Max gave himself a mental slap. God, he'd be spouting poetry next!

'I know you don't think much of *Glitz*,' Allegra was babbling on, 'but this is my career! What else am I going to do if I'm a failure as a journalist?'

'You could illustrate those children's books the way you always said you were going to.' He and his family shouldn't have been surprised when Allegra announced that she was going to follow Flick into journalism, but none of them had ever had her down as a writer. Max always thought of her drawing—quick, vivid sketches that brought a face or an animal to life in a few simple lines.

She drew back, thrown by his suggestion. 'I can't make a living as an illustrator.'

What she meant was: Flick wouldn't be pleased. Flick wanted a daughter who would follow in her footsteps, a daughter who would be a journalist on television or for some respected newspaper. Flick had no time for Allegra's 'little drawings'. Max thought it was a shame.

'It's just a few hours of your time, Max.' Allegra reverted to the problem in hand.

Would it cost him that much to help her? Max found himself thinking. She was so longing to be a success, and she deserved a break. She'd been a good friend to Libby— and to him, he acknowledged. Allegra tried so hard to be ruthless and driven like her formidable mother, but she just couldn't quite manage it. She liked to pretend that she was tough, but she was a sucker for every sob story that came along. Allegra would never admit it, but she was hampered by warmth and kindness and humour from ever pleasing Flick.

'And if I say no, I suppose you'll refuse to pretend to be my fiancée when I meet Bob Laskovski?'

Allegra looked momentarily disconcerted and Max had to stop himself rolling his eyes. It had obviously never crossed her mind that she could do more than beg him to help her. She had such a transparent expression. He could read the agonizing in her green eyes, practically hear her wondering how she could possibly threaten to go back on her promise when she'd given her word.

If he had any decency, he'd put her out of her misery and tell her that he'd do her stupid assignment, but it was fun to see how far she would go for a success she could lay at Flick Fielding's feet—and frankly, Max considered, if he was going to make an idiot of himself, he deserved some amusement in return.

'Er, yes…yes, that's right,' said Allegra after a moment and put up her chin in a futile attempt to look ruthless. 'A favour for a favour. If you don't help me with this, you can forget about me pretending to be your fiancée!'

'But you promised,' Max protested, scowling to disguise his amusement as Allegra squirmed. She was big on keeping her promises. 'If you don't come with me to that dinner, I won't get the job in Shofrar and you know how much that means to me.'

'This assignment means a lot to *me*,' Allegra pointed out, but she didn't look very comfortable about it. 'That's the deal: take it or leave it.'

'That's blackmail!' said Max.

'And your point is…?' she countered bravely.

It was all Max could do not to grin. He heaved a disgruntled sigh instead. 'Oh, all *right*. If you're going to be like that, I don't have much choice, do I? I'll take part in your precious assignment—but you'd better not have been joking about Darcy King!'

One moment he was pretending to glower at Allegra, the next his arms were full of her. Beaming, she launched herself at him, pushing him back down onto the sofa cushions as she hugged him. 'Oh, I love you, Max! Thank you, thank you, thank you!' she babbled, blizzarding kisses over his face. 'You won't regret it, I promise you. I'm going to change your life, and it's going to be perfect!'

Allegra ran from the lift as fast as she could on her polka dot slingbacks. The shoes were a fun twist to the rest of her look, a demure tweed two-piece with a short skirt and three-quarter length sleeves that channelled her inner executive-cum-fashion diva, and Allegra had been pleased when she left home. She projected confidence and style, as befitted a girl on the verge of her big break.

Until her tights laddered, that was.

If only she hadn't stopped to say hello to Mrs Gosling, but how could she run past when her elderly neighbour's face lit up at the prospect of someone to talk to? Mrs Gosling spent most of her days walking her dog, an excitable mutt called, for reasons Allegra had never understood, Derek, and that morning she had been all tangled up in the lead while Derek literally ran rings round her.

Late as she was, Allegra had had to stop and disentangle Mrs Gosling and hear about Derek's latest antics. Allegra had a friend whose small daughter Molly loved to be told how naughty Derek was, and Allegra had taken to writing out each story, exaggerating for effect, and illustrating them with little sketches of Derek's mischievous face. Molly adored them.

'You should put them into a book,' Libby had said. 'The Glorious Adventures of Derek the Dog. Mrs G would love it.'

But Allegra had shrugged the idea aside. 'They're just for Molly really.'

But that morning she had only listened with half an ear as she sorted out the lead and bent to greet Derek, who jumped at her in ecstasy.

That was the end of the tights.

Oh, God, she was so late! Red-faced and panting, Allegra practically fell through the doors into *Glitz*'s super hip offices. The editorial department sprawled over the top floor of a converted warehouse. Most days the buzz hit Allegra the moment she got out of the lift. She loved the gloss of the office, the smell of new clothes and expensive perfumes, the stark décor contrasting with the colourful scatter of accessories and shoes displayed like works of art. She loved the frantic thrum in the air, the way it was punctuated with dramatic cries and screams of excitement.

Except when Stella was present, of course, in which case everyone was very quiet unless asked to speak.

It was ominously silent when Allegra collapsed against the reception desk, a funkily curved piece of steel, and held her hand against her side.

'The editorial meeting's just started,' Lulu, the receptionist, lowered her voice and eyed Allegra with sympathy. 'You know Stella hates it when anyone is late. You'd better pretend you fell under a bus or something.'

'I might as well if I don't get in there and get my assignment,' groaned Allegra, forcing herself upright.

Smoothing down her hair, she took a deep breath and headed towards the conference room, only to be called back by Lulu's frantic whisper.

'You can't go in like that!' She pointed at Allegra's legs. 'Tights!'

Allegra clutched her head. She'd forgotten her tights

for a moment. She'd soon learnt to keep a spare pair in her bag, but changing them would take precious seconds.

'What's worse?' she asked Lulu desperately. 'Being late or laddered tights?' Lulu's astounded expression was answer enough. Clearly, Allegra shouldn't have needed to ask. 'You're right, I'd better change…'

It was Allegra's second mistake of the day. Dashing into the loos, she found Hermione, one of the marketing interns, sobbing her heart out in a cubicle, and by the time Allegra had coaxed her out and listened to her tale of woe, she was not only horribly late but had acquired two mascara smudges on the pale cashmere jumper tucked so stylishly into her skirt.

That was what you got for dispensing comforting hugs, thought Allegra bitterly as she stripped off her tights, but she was in such a hurry to get the new ones on that she managed to stick a finger through them.

'Oh, sod it!' At least this time the ladder was hidden under her skirt. Bundling the first pair into the bin, Allegra swiped at her hair. She looked completely manic, but there was nothing she could do about it now. If she didn't get into that editorial meeting, she'd lose out on the assignment. Ianthe Burrows was probably already putting forward an alternative.

'Sorry,' she mouthed generally, sliding into the conference room at last and every head swivelled to stare at her, with her flushed cheeks and tousled hair. There was a resounding silence. Stella didn't say anything but her gaze rested for a crushing few seconds on the smudges before dropping to Allegra's knees as she stood frozen just inside the room.

Against her will, Allegra found herself following her editor's gaze to where the ladder had snaked out from under her skirt. Horrified, she watched it unravel over her knee and head down her leg. She could practically hear the unzipping sound.

Why was there never a black hole around when you needed to jump into one?

'Editorial meetings start at ten,' said Stella, and Allegra cringed at the lack of inflexion in her voice.

'Yes, I know…I—' She broke off. She couldn't explain about Derek and Mrs Gosling and Hermione. Stella wouldn't care and Allegra would sound like an idiot. Even more of an idiot. 'I'm sorry,' she said instead.

A fractional incline of Stella's head served as her dismissal. The conversation returned to the latest couture debut, and Allegra slunk into a chair at the back. Pulling out notebook, pen, iPad and PDA, she willed the burning colour in her face to fade.

Fortunately, she didn't appear to have missed too much and as the discussion warmed up into articles about how to give a rock'n'roll twist to the latest looks, and the pros and cons of being friends-with-benefits, she kept her head down and let her racing pulse slow. Mindlessly doodling Derek winding Mrs Gosling up in his lead, she listened to the arguments for and against sleeping with a friend. It wasn't something she would do herself. She'd be afraid that it would spoil the friendship. Because how could it possibly be the same afterwards?

What would it have been like if Max had kissed her all those years ago? Allegra was aware of an odd jolt of heat at the thought. It had to be the thrill of the forbidden, because Max was practically her brother.

Eeuww, the very idea was disturbing at a whole load of levels! But there had been something hot and dangerous in the air that night, something that risked changing everything, and they'd both known it. Perhaps that was why they had pulled back before they did something they would both have regretted.

Because if they'd kissed, they wouldn't have stopped at a kiss, and then it really *would* have been awkward. It wasn't even as if Max was her type, Allegra thought, even as she began an absent sketch of how he had looked lying on the sofa the night before. And she certainly wasn't his. Emma was neat and dainty and blonde, a sweet little pixie, while Allegra was leggy and chaotic.

No, it was much better that they'd stayed just friends, without any jiggery-pokery, as Ianthe liked to refer to sex. They would never have been able to share the house, like now, if they'd slept together, and she wouldn't have felt comfortable asking him to take part in the assignment.

Thank God they hadn't actually kissed.

Or done anything else.

Pursing her lips, Allegra studied her drawing. It looked like Max, but the mouth wasn't *quite* right... She made a slight adjustment to his upper lip and his face sprang to life so abruptly that her heart jumped a little: steady eyes, stubborn jaw, a quiet, cool mouth. She hadn't realised how well she had memorised the angles of his cheek, the way his hair grew. She had made him look...quite attractive.

Her mouth dried and all at once she was remembering how she had hugged him in her excitement the night before. She hadn't thought about it. He was Max, and he'd just agreed to take part in something Allegra knew he was going to hate. Hugging him was the obvious thing to do.

But when her arms were around his neck and her lips pressed to his cheek, she had suddenly become aware of how solid he was, how *male*. How familiar and yet how abruptly strange. The prickle of stubble on his jaw had pressed into her cheek and she'd breathed in the clean masculine smell of him and something had twisted hard and hot in her belly.

Something that had felt alarmingly like lust. Which of course it couldn't have been because, hey, this was *Max*.

Beside her, Georgie, one of the few journalists who was as junior as Allegra, leant over and raised her eyebrows appreciatively. 'Your guy?' she mouthed.

Allegra shook her head, unaccountably flustered. 'Just a friend.'

'Right.' Georgie's smile was eloquent with disbelief.

Quickly Allegra sketched in Max's shirt, including every stripe, and the collar that was buttoned too high, and Georgie's smile faded.

'Oh.'

Quite, thought Allegra. She should do less thinking about Max's mouth and more remembering his absolutely appalling taste in shirts.

'Allegra!'

The deputy editor's voice made Allegra jerk her eyes to the front, where Stella was looking sphinx-like and Marisa, her deputy, harried. 'Could we have a moment of your attention?'

Allegra fought the impulse to say, *Yes, miss*. 'Yes, of course.'

'*Making Mr Perfect*...did you get anywhere with that?'

Clearly expecting the answer to be no, their eyes were already moving down the list, on to the next idea. This was her moment.

'Actually, yes, I did,' Allegra said and a ripple of surprise ran round the room.

'You found someone to take part?' Stella's expression was as inscrutable as ever but Allegra told herself that the very slight life of her editor's immaculate brows was a good sign.

'Yes,' she said.

'Who is he?' That was Marisa.

'The brother of a friend of mine. Max.' Why did just saying his name suddenly make her feel warm?

'What does he look like?' asked Marisa practically. 'I suppose it's too much to hope that he's a hunk?'

Allegra glanced down at her sketch of Max on the sofa: solid, steady-eyed. Ordinary. Nothing special. Her eyes rested on his mouth for a moment and there it came again without warning, a quick, disturbing spike of her pulse. She looked away.

'I wouldn't say that he was a *hunk*, exactly,' she said cautiously, 'but I think he'll brush up well.'

'Sounds promising. What's he like?'

'He's a civil engineer,' said Allegra, as if that explained everything. 'He's pretty conventional, plays rugby and doesn't have a clue about style.' She lifted her shoulders, wondering how else to describe him. 'He's just a bloke, really.'

'No girlfriend in the wings? We don't want anyone making a fuss about him spending time with Darcy.'

Allegra shook her head. 'He's just been dumped by his fiancée and he's going to work abroad soon so he's not interested in meeting anyone else at the moment. He's perfect,' she said.

'And he knows exactly what's involved?' Marisa insisted. 'He's happy to go ahead?'

Happy might be stretching it, thought Allegra, remembering uneasily how she had had to blackmail Max, but this was no time for quibbling. Her big chance was *this* close, and she was ready to seize it.

'Absolutely,' she said.

Marisa glanced at Stella, who nodded. 'In that case, you'd better get on to Darcy King and set up the first date straight away.'

CHAPTER THREE

'So this is where you work.' Max looked around him uneasily. The office was aflutter with gorgeous glossy women, all eyeing him as if they had never seen a man in a suit before and weren't sure whether to laugh or pity him.

It ought to have been gratifying to be the focus of so much undivided female attention, but Max was unnerved. He felt like a warthog who had blundered into a glasshouse full of butterflies.

Why the hell had he agreed to this stupid idea? He'd been lying there minding his own business and then Allegra had slid onto the sofa next to him and before he knew what was happening he'd been tangled up in her idea and lost in those mossy eyes and suddenly all he cared about was making her happy.

He'd even suggested his own blackmail. He must have been mad.

But the smile on Allegra's face had lit up the room and left him scrabbling for breath, and when she'd thrown herself into his arms the feel of her had left Max oddly light-headed. Her hair had trailed silkily over his face as she threw her arms round him and pressed her lips to his cheek, and the smell of her perfume had sent his mind spinning.

To Max's horror, his body had taken on a mind of its

own. Without him even being aware of what he was doing, his arms had clamped round her and for a moment he had held her against him and fought the crazy urge to slide his hands under that skimpy top and roll her beneath him.

Which would have been a very, very, very bad idea.

The next instant Allegra had pulled back, babbling excitedly about the assignment. As far as she was concerned, it had just been a sisterly hug.

That was all it *had* been, Max reminded himself sternly.

And now it seemed he was committed to the charade. 'The first thing is to smarten you up.' Allegra had gone all bossy and produced a clipboard and a list. 'Can you take an afternoon off? You're going to need a complete makeover.'

Max didn't like the sound of that. He didn't like the sound of *any* of it, come to that, but he'd given his word.

'I could take some flex leave,' he said grudgingly. He didn't want anyone at work to get wind of what was happening. That morning he'd told them that he was going to the dentist and, looking around *Glitz*'s glossy offices, he couldn't help thinking that root canal surgery might be preferable to what lay ahead.

He was going to be styled by the great Dickie himself. Allegra had impressed on Max what an honour this was. 'If he's bored or irritated, Dickie's likely to storm off, so please just be nice!' she said again as she led him between glass-walled offices and down to a studio, her sky-high heels clicking on the polished floor that she had told him was known as the runway. Apparently this was because everybody could see and comment on the outfits passing, something Max would rather not have known. He could feel all the eyes assessing his hair, his suit, his tie, his figure as he followed Allegra.

She was in businesslike mode today in skinny trousers, an animal-print top and those fearsome-looking boots, but he had to confess he preferred it when she wore a dress. She looked less...intimidating.

Plus, it showed off her legs, which were pretty spectacular.

'I'm always nice,' said Max.

Allegra cast him a look over her shoulder. 'You weren't nice about the outfit I wore last night.'

Max had been heating up a curry when she had appeared in the kitchen doorway, wearing the most extraordinary outfit. A riot of clashing colours and patterns, Max hadn't known how to describe what she was wearing, but when she'd twirled and asked what he thought, he'd made the big mistake of telling her. Words like fruit salad and dog's dinner had passed his lips.

He wouldn't be offering any more sartorial advice.

'Here we are.' Fretfully, Allegra pushed him into the studio. 'Just...nod and smile. And follow my lead,' she muttered under her breath, fixing a bright smile to her face and dragging Max towards a tiny, imperious figure with close-cropped grey hair, huge red spectacles and a red and white dotted bow tie.

'You didn't tell me I'd have to be careful not to step on him,' Max murmured and Allegra hissed at him to be quiet.

'Dickie, I'm so thrilled to be working with you,' she said, practically curtseying.

Dickie nodded regally, and they exchanged the obligatory air kiss before he turned his gaze to Max. 'And oo iz thees?' he said, his French accent so thick that Max thought he had to be putting it on.

'Max Warriner,' he said, stepping forward and shaking Dickie's hand firmly before Allegra could pretend that he was a deaf mute. He sure as hell wasn't going to kiss Dickie. 'Good to meet you,' he said briskly.

Dickie looked at his hand as if he had never had it wrung before, and then at Allegra, who smiled apologetically.

'Max is here for the *Making Mr Perfect* feature,' she said, lowering her voice. 'You know, the one with the complete makeover.'

'Ah, *oui*...' Dickie eyed Max's outfit, a perfectly serviceable suit and tie, and shuddered extravagantly. 'I see 'e needs one!'

'It's the first date tonight,' Allegra said. 'He's meeting Darcy King for cocktails at Xubu.'

Xubu, as Max had heard at length, was the latest hot ticket, the place to see and be seen, and Allegra had been desperate to go. Fortunately—for her, if not for Max—Darcy King's celebrity had opened the doors and Allegra was delighted.

'I don't see why you're so happy,' Max had said. 'You're not going.'

'Of course I have to be there,' Allegra said. 'I'm writing the article. And the photographer will be there too.'

'It doesn't sound like much of a date to me,' Max grumbled, but Allegra had brushed that aside.

'It'll be fun!'

Fun. Max shook his head, thinking about it.

'You can see how much work he needs,' Allegra was saying to Dickie, who was circling Max with much rolling of eyes and shrugging of shoulders. 'He'll need a whole new look if he's going to impress Darcy.'

'I will do what I can,' he said, plucking at Max's jacket with distaste. 'But zis, zis must go! And ze shirt—if you can call zat zing a shirt—and ze trousers...ze shoes too... Burn it all!'

'Now hold on—!' Max began, only to yelp as Allegra placed her heel firmly on his foot.

'Don't worry, Dickie. I'll take care of it. Take off your jacket,' she ordered Max out of the corner of her mouth.

'This is my work suit!' he muttered back as he took it off reluctantly. 'Don't you dare burn it.'

'Don't panic. I'll just take it home where it doesn't upset Dickie.'

'What about upsetting *me*?'

Allegra ignored him. 'What sort of look do you think for cocktails?' she asked Dickie. 'Funky? Or suave and sophisticated?'

Dickie stood back and studied Max critically, mentally stripping him of the offending clothes, and Max shifted self-consciously.

'I zink sophisticated, but with an edge,' Dickie proclaimed at last.

'Perfect,' said Allegra, the traitor. 'Not too obvious, but interesting. A look that shows Darcy he's confident enough to make his own fashion statement? A little quirky, perhaps?'

Fashion statement? Jeez...Max pinched the bridge of his nose as Allegra and Dickie talked over him. He should be checking the material testing results, or writing up the geological survey for the motorway-widening bid, not standing here like a dumb ox while they wittered on about fashion statements!

'Quirky?' Dickie considered. 'Per'aps you 'ave somezing zere...'

Max was convinced now that the French accent was put on. No one could really speak that ridiculously.

Although, for a man prepared to wear that bow tie, being ridiculous obviously wasn't a problem.

'What do you think?' Allegra asked anxiously. 'Can you do something with Max?'

For answer, Dickie spun on his heel and clapped his

hands at his minions, who had been waiting subserviently, talking to each other in hushed voices as they waited for the great man to pronounce.

'Bring out ze shirts,' he ordered.

'Behave,' Allegra whispered in Max's ear.

'I am behaving!'

'You're not. You're glaring at Dickie. Do you want me glaring at Bob Laskovski over that dinner?'

'No,' he admitted.

'Well, then.'

Allegra could see Max balking as racks of clothes surrounded him like wagons and Dickie started snapping his fingers at his assistants, who leapt forward and held up shirts side by side. Max's eyes were rolling nervously like a spooked horse and he practically had his ears flattened to his head, but Allegra stood behind Dickie and mouthed 'remember the dinner' at him until he sulkily complied and agreed to try on some shirts.

Unbuttoning his cuffs, he hooked his fingers into the back of his shirt and dragged it over his head and Allegra and Dickie both drew a sharp breath. Who would have guessed that Max had such a broad, smooth, *sexy* back beneath that dull shirt? Allegra felt quite...unsettled.

Dragging her eyes away, she made a big deal of making notes of Dickie's choices in her notebook, but her gaze kept snagging on the flex of Max's muscles as he shrugged in and out of shirts. Dickie kept turning him round— deliberately, Allegra was sure—so sometimes she saw his shoulders, sometimes his chest. And then they brought on the trousers, and there were his bare legs. Why had she never noticed before what great legs Max had?

'Allegra!' Dickie snapped his fingers in front of her face, startling her. 'What do you think?'

Allegra looked at Max. He wore a darkly flowered

button-down shirt with a striped tie that clashed and yet complemented the colours perfectly. Trousers and jacket were beautifully cut, shoes discreet. If it hadn't been for the mutinous expression, he would have looked super-cool.

'I love it,' she said. 'He's really rocking that flowered shirt.'

Max hunched a shoulder. 'I feel like a prat.'

'Well, you don't look like one for once,' she said.

'He needs an 'aircut of course,' said Dickie, eyeing Max critically.

Allegra checked her list. 'That's booked in next.'

'And a manicure.'

'Oh, no,' said Max, backing away. 'No, no, no, no, no!'

'Yes, indeed.' Allegra smiled blandly at him. 'Now don't make a fuss. It won't hurt at all.' She pretended to consult her list again. 'Although I'm not sure I can say the same for the back, sack and crack wax we've got you booked in for after the manicure…'

'Back, sack…?' Aghast, Max opened and closed his mouth before obviously spotting the dent in her cheek where she was desperately trying not to laugh. 'Why, you…' Grinning with relief, he playfully shoved at her arm.

Allegra was giggling, but tailed off when she realised everyone was standing around staring at them. How uncool of her.

She cleared her throat. 'Yes, well, take that outfit off for now. Let's do something about that hair.'

Max ran his finger around his collar. His *flowery* collar. He felt ridiculous. His hair had been washed and conditioned and cut and it was just as well it hadn't been any longer or that fool of a barber—excuse him, hairstylist—would have had it flopping all over his face. He had been shaved

too, swathed in hot towels. Actually that hadn't been too
bad—until they had slapped on some cologne without his
say-so. His eyes were still watering.

If any of his mates saw him now, or caught him stink-
ing like a tart's boudoir, he would never hear the end of
it. Thank God this was the last place he would meet anyone he knew. The dimly lit bar was crowded, but if anyone else in there was an engineer, they weren't like any
civil engineers Max had ever met. Everyone seemed to be
at least ten years younger than him and half of them were
outrageously dressed. Unbelievably, his own absurd shirt
didn't stand out at all compared to what everyone else was
wearing. He might have to forgive Allegra for it after all.
He'd been so certain that she'd deliberately manoeuvred
Dickie into choosing the flowery shirt as a joke.

'Isn't this place fab?' Across the table, Allegra was
bright-eyed as she surveyed the crowd. Dom, the photographer, was sitting next to her and together they were
keeping up a running commentary on celebrities they had
spotted and what everyone was wearing. Max had tuned
out after a while. He hoped Darcy King would turn up
soon and make this purgatory worthwhile.

'Don't look now…' Allegra leant forward with a little
squeal of excitement '…but that's Chris O'Donnell sitting
behind you!'

'No! Not Chris! Squeeeee!'

She looked at him. 'You don't know who Chris
O'Donnell is, do you?' Without waiting for his reply, she
turned to Dom. 'He doesn't know who Chris O'Donnell is.'

Dom stared at Max. 'You just jetted in from Mars or
something, man?'

'Chris O'Donnell is the ultimate bad boy rocker,' said
Allegra, apparently shocked to her core by the depths of
Max's ignorance. 'He just got voted sexiest man in the

country, and he'd certainly have had my vote...' She sighed wistfully.

Max raised his brows. 'I didn't know you had a taste for bad boy rockers, Legs. Not your usual type, surely? I don't see your mother approving.'

Allegra flushed. 'I wouldn't want him as a boyfriend or anything, but you've got to admit he's smokin' hot...'

'So have you told Flick about your major new assignment?' Max said, not wanting to get into a discussion about which men Allegra thought were hot. He was fairly sure the list wouldn't include a civil engineer, flowery shirt or not.

Not that he cared about that. It was just uncomfortable to talk about that kind of stuff with someone he'd known for so long. It would be like discussing sex with his sister.

'I rang her last night.' Allegra's brightness dimmed slightly.

'Was she pleased to hear about your big break?'

'Well, you know Flick.' Her smile was painful to watch and Max cursed himself for asking. He should have known Flick would disappoint her. 'She did say "Well done" when I explained that it might mean a promotion if the article was a success. But she's writing about the political implications of the economic crisis; you can't blame her for not being impressed by my piece on whether it's possible to create the perfect boyfriend. I suspect she thinks it's a bit silly.'

Max had thought precisely the same thing but now, perversely, he was outraged at Flick's dismissal of Allegra's assignment. 'Did you tell her all that stuff you told me, about how these were the kind of issues that really matter to a lot of young women?'

Allegra sighed. 'I don't think boyfriend trouble quite ranks with the global downturn in the economy in my mother's scheme of things.' She squared her shoulders, sat up straighter. 'And she's right, of course. I should take more interest in political issues.'

She was nothing if not loyal to her mother, Max thought, still irrationally annoyed by Flick's response. Would it have killed her to have encouraged her daughter for once? Poor Allegra tried so hard to get her mother's approval. She had to want it bad to feign an interest in politics, given that he'd never heard her or Libby utter a word on the subject.

And she was going to find it hard, as demonstrated by the fact that barely had her resolve to be more politically aware fallen from her lips than her attention was caught by a girl teetering past in ludicrously high shoes. 'Omigod, I am totally stealing that vampire chic look!'

Max was obscurely pleased to see her revert to her frivolous self. 'Vampire chic?' he echoed, knowing the disbelief in his voice would annoy her, and sure enough, she gave him the flat-eyed look she and Libby had perfected when they were twelve.

Back to normal. Good.

'You just don't get it, do you?' she said. 'Look at you! We bring you to the hottest place in town, and you sit there like you were wishing you were in some grotty pub!'

'There's no "like" about it. I *am* wishing I was in a pub.'

'Here, have a drink.' Allegra passed him the drinks list. 'Maybe that'll cheer you up—and no, you can't have a pint.'

Morosely, Max scanned the list and choked when he saw the prices. 'They want *how* much for a cocktail?'

'Don't panic, you're not paying for the drinks,' she said. 'But, in all other respects, this is a real date, so start looking as if you're looking forward to meeting Darcy, not as if you're waiting to have your eyes poked out with a sharp stick.'

She shook her head as Max tried to ease the tightness around his neck. Dickie had a throttling way with a tie. 'Relax!' she said, leaning across the table to slap his hand away from his throat, and the scent of her perfume momentarily clouded Max's brain.

'You're so repressed,' she told him as he blinked the disturbing awareness away. 'Now listen, you're going to meet Darcy any minute and you're going to have to make an effort. This is your first task. You need to make sure she likes you enough to accept your invitation to dinner cooked by you, which is your second task.'

'You've explained all this,' said Max grouchily.

'And, just in case you were thinking of falling at the first hurdle so that you don't have to carry on, I'll just remind you that we haven't had that dinner with your boss yet.'

Why had he ever put the idea of blackmail into her head? She had taken to it like a natural. He'd created a monster.

'Remember, you're interested in Darcy, not in a lingerie model,' Allegra carried on bossily. 'Ask her questions but don't interrogate her—and don't expect her to take all the burden of the conversation either.'

'I've been on dates before, you know.'

Allegra ignored that. 'She'll be hoping to meet someone interesting and interested, someone charming and witty who can make her laugh, but who's got some old-fashioned manners—don't forget to stand up when she arrives—and who can make her feel safe but sexy and desirable at the same time.'

'And I'm going to be doing all of this with you listening in and Dom here taking pictures?'

'You'll hardly notice us after a while,' she assured him, then straightened as Dom nudged her. 'And here she comes! Good luck,' she mouthed to Max as he adjusted his tie and slid out of the banquette to greet Darcy.

He couldn't help staring. Spectacular was the only word. Of course he'd seen photos before, blown up across billboards or plastered across magazines, but in the flesh Darcy was breathtaking. She glowed with sex appeal, from her artfully tumbled blonde hair to the bee-stung mouth and the voluptuous body.

'Your tongue's hanging out,' Allegra said in his ear, and Max shut his mouth with a snap.

'You must be Max,' said Darcy in the famously husky voice and Max unscrambled his mind.

'I am. It's good to meet you, Darcy,' he said and stuck out his hand, but she only laughed and brushed it aside as she moved forward to kiss him on the cheek, enveloping him in a haze of perfume and allure.

'Let's not be formal,' she said while every man in the room watched him enviously. 'I hear we're going to be great friends!'

Dry-mouthed, Max stood back to usher her into the banquette. 'It sounds like you know more than I do,' he said with an accusing glance at Allegra, who was greeting Darcy cheerfully. What else hadn't she told him?

'Don't worry, darling,' said Darcy, patting his hand. 'It's going to be fun.'

Darcy and Max were getting on like the proverbial fire in a match factory. Allegra told herself she should be pleased that it was going so well. She took a gulp of the sparkling water she'd ordered as she was supposed to be working.

Darcy was obviously enjoying herself. She threw her head back and laughed her glorious laugh. She propped her chin on her hands and leant forwards, as if the famous cleavage needed attention drawn to it. She flirted with those impossibly long lashes and ran her fingers up and down Max's arm. Max, unsurprisingly, wasn't complaining.

He was doing much better than she had expected, Allegra had to admit. After that stunned moment—and she couldn't honestly blame him for that—he had recovered quickly and, while he wasn't exactly *charming,* he had a certain assurance that came from not caring what anybody else thought of him, and a kind of dry humour that seemed to be going down well with Darcy anyway.

Which Allegra was delighted about, naturally.

No, really, she was. Personally, she didn't think it was necessary for Darcy to touch him *quite* so often, but Darcy was obviously the tactile type. Not her fault that Allegra's fingers were twitching with the longing to reach across the table and slap her hand from Max's arm.

Who would have thought Max would brush up so well too? She'd thought he would dig in his heels at the flowery shirt but, apart from a few fulminating glances sent her way he'd clearly decided to honour his part of the agreement. Unlikely as it was, the shirt suited him beautifully. Something about the fabrics and the exquisite cut of the garments gave him a style he had certainly never possessed before.

It would take more than a shirt to turn him into an über hunk, of course, but Allegra had to allow that he didn't look as ordinary as he usually did.

It was amazing what a difference a good haircut made, too. She found herself noticing all sorts of things about him that she had never noticed before: the line of his jaw, the crease in his cheek, the uncompromising brows.

Vaguely disturbed, Allegra bent her head over her notebook. She was listening to the conversation between Max and Darcy as unobtrusively as possible and scribbling notes for the article she would write up when the final task was completed.

The article that could change her career and put her in a position to apply for jobs on magazines with a little more gravitas. If she got it right.

So why was she letting herself be distracted by the way Max's smile had suddenly started catching at the corner of her eye, the way it had suddenly started making her pulse kick as if it had startled her?

He was only smiling, for God's sake. She *wanted* him to be smiling at Darcy. She was supposed to be pleased with the way it was going, not feeling cross.

Darcy was telling Max a long story about the house she was having built, and he was offering advice about foundations and geological surveys. He'd obviously forgotten her advice about being witty and charming, but Darcy was hanging on his every word.

Disgruntled, Allegra gave up listening after a while. She wasn't going to fill her article with engineering talk, however fascinating Darcy might find it. Dom had taken his pictures and left some time before, and she let her pen drift: Derek the Dog dancing on his hind legs, Mrs G tipsy on cocktails, Flick smiling proudly—Allegra had to imagine that one.

Then she sketched Darcy leaning forward, lips parted breathlessly, and Max himself. But somehow she found herself drawing the Max she knew, the Max who wore a crummy polo shirt buttoned too high at the neck and lay on the absurdly feminine sofa, king of the remote, and she felt a pang of something she chose not to identify.

'Hey, those are great!' Darcy leant across the table and plucked the notebook away before Allegra had a chance to react.

She studied the drawings, chuckling. 'Who's the cute

dog? Look, Max, that's you...' Her smile faltered as she took in the polo shirt. 'At least...?'

Max peered at the sketch. 'Yep, looks like me.'

Allegra was blushing furiously. 'They're just doodles...'

'No, really, they're very good,' said Darcy. 'You clever thing.' She tapped a finger on the picture of her. 'You've caught me exactly, hasn't she, Max?'

'It's unmistakably you, but a drawing can't really capture your charm,' he said and Darcy laughed her trademark husky laugh, delighted, while Allegra concentrated on not throwing up.

If she wasn't much mistaken, Max was *flirting*. He must really like Darcy. Perhaps it was time to leave them alone. Ignoring the sinking feeling in her stomach, she took her notebook back from Darcy. 'I should go.'

'Don't go yet.' To her surprise, rather than wanting to get rid of her, Max handed her the drinks list. 'If you've finished working, you might as well have a proper drink.'

'Absolutely,' said Darcy with a sunny smile. 'You deserve it for setting up this article. I just know we're going to have a good time.' Her fingers teased Max's shoulder and Allegra's fingers tightened around the menu. 'I can't believe Max here hasn't been snapped up already, can you?'

'It's beyond comprehension,' Allegra agreed, but then made the mistake of glancing at Max. A smile hovered around his mouth and, for no reason she could name, her mouth dried.

'Try something with a ridiculous name,' he said, deadpan, and nodded at the drinks list. 'I'm longing to make a fool of myself ordering for you.'

Allegra swallowed and wrenched her gaze away to concentrate fiercely on the drinks list. Could she be coming down with something? She felt feverish and twitchy, and a nerve was jumping under her eye.

The list kept swimming in front of her eyes and she frowned in an effort to focus, but whenever she did the only cocktails that jumped out at her were called things like Screaming Orgasm or Wet Kiss. This was supposed to be fun. She should take Max up on his challenge and make him order something silly.

Why couldn't she grin and say: *I'd like a Sloe Screw Against the Wall, please, Max? Could I have Sex on the Beach?*

But all at once her throat was thick and she was having trouble swallowing. She handed the list back without meeting his eyes. 'I'll...er...have a martini, please.'

'Chicken,' said Max, beckoning over a waitress.

Darcy started to tell Allegra about a shoot she'd been on the day before. She knew Dickie and Stella and a host of other people at *Glitz*, and she was so friendly that it was impossible to dislike her, in spite of the way she kept flirting with Max, little touches on his arm, his shoulder, his hair. Every now and then her hand would disappear under the table and Allegra didn't want to think about what she was touching down there.

Allegra kept her attention firmly focused on Darcy's face, which was easier than being stupidly conscious of Max sitting next to Darcy and not looking nearly as out of place as he should have done. More and more, Allegra was convinced that she was sickening for something. She didn't feel herself at all. She was glad when the drinks arrived, but she drank hers a little too quickly and, before she knew what had happened, Darcy was beckoning for another one.

'You're one behind us,' she said gaily.

CHAPTER FOUR

So ALLEGRA HAD another and then she and Darcy agreed to have another. Why had she been so uptight earlier? She was having a great time now, exchanging disastrous date stories with Darcy while Max sat back, folded his arms and watched them indulgently.

'Like you've never had a disastrous date,' Allegra accused him, enunciating carefully so as not to slur her words.

'What about this one?' said Max.

'We're talking about *real* dates,' she said indignantly.

Darcy nodded along. 'When your heart sinks five minutes in and you spend the rest of the evening trying to think of an excuse to leave early.'

'Or, worse, when you really like someone and you realise they're just not that into *you*,' said Allegra glumly.

A funny look swept across Max's face. 'I've got no idea what you're talking about,' he said.

Darcy had already moved on. 'I blame my father,' she said. 'He's spoilt me for other men. None of my boyfriends has ever been able to live up to him.'

'You're lucky to have a father,' Allegra said wistfully.

Her birth certificate just showed her mother's name. Flick refused to talk about Allegra's father. 'He was a mistake,' was all she would ever say and turn the subject.

When she was a little girl, Allegra had dreamed that her father would turn up one day and claim his daughter. She could never decide if she'd rather he was a movie star or the prince of some obscure European principality. Usually she opted for the latter; she thought she would make a good princess.

But no father ever came for her.

Thinking about fathers always made Allegra feel unloved and unwanted. If she wasn't careful, she'd start blubbing, so she smiled instead and lifted her glass. 'Oh,' she said, peering owlishly into it when she discovered it was empty, 'let's have another round.'

'I think you've had enough,' said Max, signalling for the bill instead. 'It's time to go home.'

'I don't want to go home. I want another martini.'

Max ignored her and put a surprisingly strong hand under her elbow to lift her, still protesting, to her feet. 'Can I get you a taxi, Darcy?'

'You're sweet,' Darcy said, 'but I might stay for a while.' She waved at someone behind them, and Allegra turned to follow her gaze. 'I'm just going to say hello to Chris.'

'Omigod, you know *Chris O'Donnell?* Allegra squeaked, but Max had already said a brisk goodbye and was propelling her towards the exit while she gawked over her shoulder in a really uncool way.

'What are you *doing*?' she complained. 'I was *this* close to meeting Chris O'Donnell.'

'You're completely sozzled,' said Max, pushing her through the doors. 'You wouldn't even remember him tomorrow.'

'I so would,' she said sulkily, and then reeled when the cold hit her. It was September still but there was an unmistakable snap of autumn in the air. If it hadn't been for his firm grip on her arm, she might have keeled right over.

Max looked down at her shoes—they were adorable peep-toes in a dusty pink suede with vertiginous heels— but he didn't look impressed. 'We'd better get a taxi,' he sighed.

Allegra's head was spinning alarmingly and she blinked in a vain attempt to focus. 'You'll never get a taxi round here,' she said but Max just propped her against a wall while he put his fingers in his mouth and whistled for a taxi. Annoyingly, one screeched to a halt straight away.

Having taken up position by the wall, it was harder than Allegra had anticipated to get over to the taxi. In the end Max had to manoeuvre her inside, where she collapsed over the seat in an undignified sprawl. She managed to struggle upright in a brave attempt to recover her dignity, but then she couldn't find her seat belt.

Her fumbling was interrupted by Max, muttering under his breath, who reached across her to locate the belt and clip it into place. His head was bent as he fiddled with the clip, and Allegra's spinning head jarred to a halt with the horrifyingly clear urge to touch his hair.

Clenching her fists into her skirt to stop her hands lifting of their own accord, she sucked in a breath and pressed her spine away from him into the seat, desperate to put as much space between them as she could.

'I think it all went well tonight,' she said. The idea was to sound cool and formal, to show Max that she wasn't nearly as sloshed as he seemed to think, but perfectly capable of carrying on a rational conversation. Unfortunately her voice came out wheezy, as if she had missed out on her share of oxygen.

Allegra cleared her throat and tried again. 'Darcy's lovely, isn't she?'

Yes, she was. Max had to agree. Darcy was a fantasy come to life, in fact. She was gorgeous and sexy and friendly and sweet-natured. So why hadn't he been able to relax and enjoy himself?

Max scowled at the back of the taxi driver's head as he fastened his own seat belt. Beside him, Allegra was still burbling on about what a great evening it had been, and how nice Darcy was. She obviously hadn't spent the entire evening being distracted.

Darcy was very touchy-feely, that was for sure. Max had been aware of her fingers trailing up and down his arm and over his thigh, but how could he enjoy it when Allegra was sitting opposite, scribbling notes in her book as if he were some kind of experiment she was observing?

It was mad. He, Max Warriner, had Darcy King *right beside him*, Darcy King *flirting with him*, and he couldn't concentrate. He was too aware of Allegra, eyeing him critically, her mouth pursed consideringly while she watched Darcy paw him. It obviously didn't bother her in the least.

It wasn't even as if there was any comparison between the two women. Darcy was lush, flirty, sex personified, while Allegra was slender, too thin really. So why did he keep remembering how it had felt when she hugged him? She'd been so soft and so warm, and her fragrance had enveloped him, and every bit of blood had drained from his head.

'And you were brilliant too,' said Allegra indistinctly. Her head kept lolling forward and Max had a sudden and very weird compulsion to unclip her seat belt again and ease her down so that she could lie with her head in his lap and sleep all the way home.

The taxi turned a corner and Allegra leant right over towards him before the car straightened and he caught the tantalising scent of her hair before she was thrown upright again. 'I feel a bit strange,' she said in a small voice.

'You'll be fine when you've had something to eat,' said Max bracingly, and she made a face.

'Ugh…I couldn't face eating anything.'

'Of course you could. We'll pick up a pizza on the way home.'

'Pizza? Are you mad?' Allegra demanded, roused out of her dopey state. 'Do you know how many calories there are in every slice?'

'You've just been guzzling cocktails,' he pointed out. 'A bit of pizza isn't going to make much difference after that. Besides, you're skinny enough. You could do with putting on a bit of weight, if you ask me.'

Allegra just looked at him pityingly. 'You've never worked in women's fashion, have you?'

'And I dare say I never will,' said Max without the slightest regret.

'Oh, I don't know. Now you've worn a flowery shirt, who knows what will happen?'

'That's what I'm afraid of,' he said glumly.

There was a silence, not uncomfortable. Lost in thought, Allegra was looking out of the window at the imposing façades along Piccadilly. It was long past the rush hour, but the traffic was still inching through the lights. They could do with a decent traffic pattern analysis, Max thought, doing his best to keep his mind off the tempting line of Allegra's throat or the coltishly sprawled legs revealed by the short flirty skirt he had been trying not to notice all evening. It was a pale mint-green, made of some kind of floaty, gauzy stuff, and she wore it with a camisole and a pale cardigan that just begged to be stroked. Darcy had cooed over its softness when she reached over and ran her hand down Allegra's sleeve, exclaiming the way women did over each other's clothes. Max had watched, his throat dry, and he'd fought the weird compulsion to push Darcy aside and stroke Allegra himself.

It was all very unsettling. He'd never given any thought to what she was wearing before—other than to boggle at the shoes she wore sometimes—so why was he suddenly acutely aware of the way her skirt shifted over her thighs when she sat down, or how some silky fabric lay against her skin?

Her face was partly turned away, and what he could see of her cheek and jaw was soft in the muted orange glow from the street. It was just this stupid assignment of hers, throwing them together in a way they'd never been before, Max decided. The sooner they got back to normal the better.

Ignoring Allegra's protests, Max ordered a large pizza the moment they got in. Allegra collapsed onto the sofa, rubbing her poor toes and moaning about the calorie count, but her mouth watered when the pizza arrived.

'I suppose I could have a tiny slice,' she said.

They sat on the floor, leaning back against the sofa with the pizza box between them. Allegra lifted a slice and took a bite, pulling at the stringy cheese with her fingers as she chewed. She would regret it in the morning, but God, it tasted good! And Max was right; she was already feeling better.

Closing her eyes, she pushed the calorie count from her mind and savoured the taste and the contrasting textures: the smoothness of the tomato paste, the chunky onions, the rubbery cheese, the bite of chorizo.

'Mmm...' She pushed a stray piece of cheese into her mouth and opened her eyes only to find Max watching her with an odd expression. 'What?' she asked.

'Nothing,' he said, looking away. 'You ought to eat more often if you enjoy it that much.'

'Are you kidding? I'd be the size of a house!'

But in that brief moment when their eyes had met, something had shifted in the air between them. Something that reminded Allegra uneasily of the night when Max had *not* kissed her.

The last thing she ought to be remembering right now.

She really shouldn't have had so many martinis. No wonder she was feeling so odd. Why did she suddenly feel as if she had to search around for something to say to break the silence? This was Max. She'd never needed to make conversation with him. Apart from that night, the one she wasn't thinking about. But now the silence between them thrummed with an unease that left her heart thumping inexplicably.

To distract herself, she picked up another piece of pizza. 'You'll have to do better than pizza when you invite Darcy over to supper.' There went her voice again, wobbling ridiculously up and down the register.

'I'm inviting Darcy to supper?'

'It's your second task,' she reminded him through a mouthful of pizza. 'The perfect boyfriend is not only sophisticated enough to enjoy cocktails, he's also a home-loving guy who can cook a delicious meal.'

'Well, I hope Darcy likes a roast, because that's all I can do.'

'Better make it a nut roast. She's a vegetarian.'

Max stared at her in consternation. 'A *vegetarian?* You didn't tell me that!'

'I didn't want to bamboozle you with too much information at once.'

'You mean you knew I'd back out,' he grumbled.

'Come on, Max, you make it sound like she eats babies!

They're only vegetables. I'm sure you can manage something. It doesn't have to be complicated, but you do need to cook it yourself. Libby's got a cookbook with some good recipes in it.'

Glad of an excuse to get away from the oddly strained atmosphere in the sitting room, Allegra pushed the last piece of pizza into her mouth and jumped up. Licking her fingers, she went into the kitchen and came back bearing the recipe book.

'Goat's cheese ravioli…that sounds nice,' she said as she flicked through the pages. 'Roasted vegetable tart… leek risotto…there's loads in here you could try.'

She handed the recipe book to Max, who looked through it without enthusiasm. 'Emma used to do all the cooking,' he said.

'Maybe she would have liked it if you'd done more,' said Allegra.

'Emma loves cooking,' he said defensively.

'I'm sure she does, but that doesn't mean that she wouldn't have appreciated it if you took a turn occasionally. You know, this is exactly the kind of thing you should get out of this exercise,' Allegra went on, warming to her theme. She was feeling more herself again, thank goodness. 'You've got a real chance here to learn how to please her. To show her that you've changed, that you're prepared to make an effort for her. I don't think you should give up.'

Max eyed her suspiciously. 'You seem very keen for me to get back together with Emma.'

'I'm keen for you to be happy,' she corrected him. 'And you seemed happy when you were with her.' It was true. Not to mention that *she* had been happier when he had been with Emma. There had been none of this uneasy awareness then. Max had just been someone to come across at the occasional family party—his family, not

hers, naturally; Flick wasn't big on jolly get-togethers—
to share a quick, spiky exchange for old times' sake and
forget about until the next time.

It wasn't that Max had been dull, but his life was so far
removed from Allegra's that she had never really *looked*
at him until that awkward evening when something had
clicked in the air, as surely as a bolt sliding into place.
She'd been able to convince herself that that had been an
aberration, especially when he'd met Emma, but now…
it was making her nervous. She shouldn't be feeling jit-
tery around Max. She shouldn't be noticing his mouth or
his hands or the fact that beneath that shirt he wore was a
lean, muscled body. It was all *wrong.*

The sooner he got back together with Emma the better.
Then everything could go back to normal.

And clearly Max thought the same.

'I *was* happy with her,' he remembered. 'We had so
much in common. We were friends! I still can't believe
she'd give up everything she had for some guy she'd only
known a few weeks.'

'It won't last,' Allegra said confidently.

'I didn't realise you were a great expert on passion!'

She forgave him the snide comment. Emma was still a
very sore point, that much was clear.

'I've done my share of falling passionately in love, only
to wake up one day and think: what am I doing?' she told
him. 'Trust me, Emma will do the same, and you need to
be there when she does. You need to show her that you've
listened to what she said and that you're prepared to do
whatever it takes to get her back.'

'Don't tell me: you're writing the *Glitz* agony column
this month?'

'You may mock,' said Allegra with dignity, 'but it's
good advice. If you really want Emma back, you should

start paying attention and, in the meantime, get in touch with her. Send a text or something, no pressure.'

'And say what?' asked Max, who was at least listening, if unwillingly.

'Just say you're thinking of her,' said Allegra. 'That'll be enough for now.'

'I can't believe you're making me do this.' Max was in a grouchy mood and Allegra had to practically push him along the street towards the dance studio.

She had booked a private lesson so that Max could learn how to waltz before the costume ball. Darcy was thrilled by the idea, a fact that Allegra had yet to pass on to Max. 'I can't wait,' she'd confided to Allegra. 'I've never been out with anyone who knew how to dance properly.'

It would be Max's hardest test, but Allegra was determined that he would succeed. It wouldn't be much of an article if she had to report that he could manage some chit-chat over a drink but that when it came to really making an effort he had flunked out.

Besides, she was longing to learn how to waltz herself. Not that she had anyone to waltz with, but maybe her prince would be waiting at the ball. He'd be tall, dark and handsome, and unaccountably stood up by his date, and he would twirl her around the ballroom in his arms while Max was impressing Darcy with some nifty footwork.

Allegra's fantasy ground to a halt as Max balked at the sign on the door, an unfortunate pink decorated with fairies.

'We're not going in here?'

She could practically see him digging his heels into the concrete and she took his arm in a firm grip. 'There are no fairies inside, I promise. You just have to be brave and get past the door!'

Grumbling, Max let her manoeuvre him inside and up some stairs to the dance studio. Afraid that he would conveniently forget the arrangement, Allegra had gone to waylay him outside his office after work. She'd hung around on the pavement, feeling conspicuous in her pencil skirt, cropped jacket and funky boots, and deeply unimpressed by the style standards in civil engineering. Male or female, everyone who came out seemed to be safely dressed in sensible dark suits.

Allegra had twisted her ankle out to admire her studded suede boots. She would hate to work anywhere that dull. She hadn't seen a single outfit with any colour or flair. If this was the environment where Max spent his days, it was no wonder he had such appalling dress sense.

Hugging her arms together against the cool autumn breeze, she'd shifted from foot to foot as she kept an eye on the door. If Max didn't come out soon, she would have to go in and get him.

And suddenly there he was.

He'd pushed through the doors with two other men. They were identically dressed in suits and ties. Max wasn't the tallest or the best-looking, but for some reason Allegra's heart kicked when she caught sight of him. He was laughing at something one of the others said as he turned away, lifting a hand in farewell, and he ran lightly down the steps, scanning the street as he went.

He was looking for her. The realisation made her heart give another odd little jump and she was smiling foolishly when his gaze crossed hers, only to stop and swing back and meet her gaze. Their eyes locked with what Allegra could have sworn was an audible click and for a moment it was as if a question trembled in the air between them.

Then Max rolled his eyes and came towards her and

the moment was broken. He was just Max—staid, conventional Max. Libby's brother. Nothing more.

'I see you didn't trust me to make my own way to the dance studio,' he said as he came up.

Allegra felt as if she ought to kiss him on the cheek or something, but all at once she felt ridiculously shy. She wouldn't have hesitated at work, but she was on Max's ground now and it seemed too intimate to give him a casual hug.

So she kept her arms wrapped around herself and turned to walk beside him instead. 'You've got to admit that you didn't seem very keen when I reminded you about the dance lesson this morning,' she said. 'You'd rather stick pins in your eyes, you said.'

'I'm here, aren't I?'

'Only because I just happened to mention at the same time that I could still pull out of the dinner with your boss.'

'Yes, who would have guessed you'd turn into such a proficient blackmailer?'

Allegra spread her hands. 'We all have to use the talents we have,' she said modestly. 'I'm helping you with the dinner for Darcy too, don't forget. I believe in the carrot and stick approach.'

'I'm still waiting for some carrot,' said Max.

Now she put the flat of her hand against Max's back and pushed him into the studio. It was a large room with two mirrored walls and the faintly sweaty smell of packed exercise classes.

At least today they had the place to themselves. Allegra introduced Max to Cathy, the dance instructor she had hired at huge expense. A TV veteran, Cathy was famous for bringing unlikely celebrities up to scratch on the dancing front, but it was soon obvious that Max was going to be her biggest challenge.

'It's like trying to move a block of wood around the floor,' she complained. 'Allegra, you come and dance with him and see if he's more relaxed with you.'

It was exactly what Allegra had been hoping for. She leapt up and took her place in the middle of the empty floor with Max, but the moment she put one hand on his shoulder and the other in his palm, awkwardness gripped her. She hadn't anticipated how close Max would feel, how intimate it would seem to be standing together, holding each other.

'Right, Max, remember what I told you: you're stepping to the top of the box, and Allegra, you go back,' said Cathy, prowling around them. 'Off we go. One, two, three…top of the box, slide across, back…one, two, three…'

Allegra's mouth was dry, but she took a deep breath and tried to remember the instructions. She kept her eyes fixed on a spot behind Max's shoulder, which made it easier not to think about how warm and firm his fingers were, or the way his hand at her waist seemed to be sizzling through her top. Out of the corner of her eye, she could still see the edge of his jaw, rigid with concentration. It was very distracting and she kept forgetting where her feet were supposed to go.

'Stop! I can't stand it!' Cathy shrieked eventually, and Max and Allegra sprang apart with a mixture of relief and embarrassment.

Cathy heaved a dramatic sigh. 'I thought you told me you and Max were friends?' she said to Allegra.

Allegra and Max looked at each other. 'We are…sort of.'

'Sort of?'

'We've known each other a long time,' Max said after a moment.

Cathy arched an eyebrow. 'You surprise me. You were holding each other as if you'd never met before.' She sighed and regarded them both severely. 'Hug each other,' she ordered.

'What?'

'Hug each other,' Cathy repeated with exaggerated patience as Allegra and Max both did double takes.

'You mean…?' Allegra gestured vaguely, prompting another big sigh from Cathy.

'I mean put your arms around each other and squeeze. You know how to hug, don't you?'

'What's the object of the exercise?' asked Max, who clearly didn't want to get any closer than Allegra did.

'I want you to relax and feel comfortable with each other. A hug will help you get over any awkwardness. Well, go on,' she said when neither of them moved.

Clearing her throat, Allegra turned reluctantly to face Max. 'Sorry,' she mouthed at him and Max rolled his eyes in reply.

They had a couple of false starts where they stepped towards each other only to bang their heads together, or find their arms so awkwardly positioned that they had to pull apart and start again, but they were laughing by that stage and on the third try they got it right.

Allegra ended up with her arms around Max's waist, while he held her pressed against him. It felt as if they had slotted into place. Max was just the right height. Allegra fitted comfortably against him, her eyes level with his jaw, and if she turned her head, she could rest her face into his throat.

He had discarded his jacket but was still wearing a shirt and tie. The shirt was a very dull pale blue and the tie totally uninteresting, but Allegra had to admit that he smelt nice, of clean cotton and clean male. It was surprisingly reassuring being able to lean into his solid strength and feel that he wouldn't shift or topple over.

It had been another frenetic day at *Glitz* and Allegra had spent most of it galloping up and down the corridors and being screamed at. They were putting the next issue to bed and tension was running higher than usual, which made it stratospheric. It was as if the whole office was suffering from PMT.

But now she was being forced to rest against Max for a minute or two. In spite of herself, Allegra let out a little sigh and relaxed. It was weird, but being held by him like this felt…safe.

'Good,' said Cathy. 'Now squeeze each other tighter.'

Obediently, Allegra tightened her arms around Max's back as he pulled her closer, and suddenly it didn't feel safe at all.

Suddenly it felt dangerous, as if the floor had dropped away beneath her feet and left her teetering on the edge of a dizzying drop. The urge to turn into Max and cling to him was so strong that Allegra couldn't breathe with it. Her chest was tight, her pulse booming with an alarmed awareness of him. He held her rigidly and his body was hard—and when Allegra shifted uneasily against him she realised that—*oh?*—it wasn't just his chest that was hard.

Oh.

Before she had a chance to work out what she felt about that, Cathy was clapping her hands.

'Right, let's try again,' she said briskly and Max practically shoved Allegra away from him. His body might have been enjoying being pressed up against her, but his mind obviously hadn't. He scowled as Cathy ordered them back into position.

'Remember what I told you about the box step?' she said as Max and Allegra took hold of each other awkwardly, careful to keep a gap between them. 'Step to the top of the box, slide your feet together, step back, slide together… Off you go!'

It was easier without the distraction of being pressed right against him, Allegra told herself. That flood of heat had just been a physical reaction, exactly as Max's had been. It was what happened when you squashed a man and a woman together. It didn't *mean* anything.

'No, no!' Cathy threw up her hands. 'Max, you go *forward*, Allegra you're stepping *back*! Now, try again, and this time try and concentrate on what you're doing.'

Right, concentrate. Allegra stifled a nervous giggle as she fluffed it again, and Max muttered under his breath.

Cathy sighed.

They set off again, and managed two sides of the box before Max trod heavily on Allegra's foot, making her yelp, at which point they both started laughing. It was partly embarrassment, partly relief that the awful awareness had dissipated.

Cathy was less amused. 'You're both hopeless,' she said when their time was up. 'If you want Max to impress Darcy at the ball, you're going to have to practice. At least master the basic steps and we can try and add some turns next week.'

CHAPTER FIVE

'TURNS?' MAX GRUMBLED as they slunk out. 'You mean we have to go round and round as well as backwards and forwards?'

'It's a lot harder than it looks,' Allegra agreed, winding her scarf around her throat. 'I've waltzed so often in my fantasies that I thought I'd be quite good at it. I can't believe I was so crap,' she said despondently.

'In your fantasy you don't dance with me, that's why,' said Max, feeling obscurely guilty about spoiling the waltz for her.

'True.' She perked up a little as they headed down the street. 'I'd be much better with my Regency duke.'

'Your what?'

'The duke who waltzes me out on the terrace, begs me to become his duchess and ravishes me,' said Allegra as if it was the most normal thing in the world. 'I told you about my fantasy.'

'You didn't mention any dukes.'

'I think he probably *is* a duke,' she said, having considered the matter. 'He's got a dreadful reputation as a rake, of course, but underneath he's deeply honourable.'

'He's not very honourable if he ravishes you right outside a crowded ballroom,' Max pointed out.

'You're such a nitpicker,' she said without heat.

Max shook his head. 'I can't figure you out, Legs. One minute you're obsessed with fashion or celebrity gossip, the next you're fantasising about dancing with dead aristocrats.'

And that was before you took into account the sweet and funny Allegra who drew cute cartoon animals, or the one who tried so hard and so unsuccessfully to be cool and high-minded so that she could please her demanding mother. The one who fretted constantly about her weight or the one who sat on the floor and ate pizza with relish.

It was only since moving into the house that Max had come to realise that there was more to Allegra than he had thought. If he'd been asked to describe her before then he would have said sweet, a bit scatty, a bit screwed up by her mother.

And now…now he was learning new things about her every day. Like the way she left the bathroom a tip, the way her face lit up when she smiled. Like the smell of her perfume. The way she tilted her chin.

The way she felt. Max's mouth dried at the memory of that ridiculous hug Cathy had insisted on. After a couple of false starts, Allegra had fitted into him as if she belonged there, and his senses had reeled alarmingly at the feel of her slenderness pressed against him.

And it wasn't just his senses that had reacted. Max shifted his shoulders uncomfortably in his jacket, remembering how aroused he had been. Hold her tighter, that fool Cathy had said. What was he supposed to do when a soft, warm woman was melting into him and her perfume filled his head and it was all he could do to stop his hands sliding under that silky top, rucking up that sexy skirt so that he could run them hungrily over her long thighs?

This was all Emma's fault. If they'd still been together, he wouldn't have been sex-starved, and he certainly wouldn't have been thinking about Allegra like some kind of pervert.

She was lucky that treading on her toes was all he had done.

At least it had been easier once they'd started laughing. It was a relief to know that Allegra couldn't dance for toffee either. When he wasn't wanting to rip her clothes off, he and Allegra got on much better than he had expected.

She'd been teaching him how to cook so that he could impress Darcy, and kept coming back from *Glitz* laden with ingredients and advice from the food editor. Max wasn't learning much, but he enjoyed leaning against the worktop and watching her face as she chopped enthusiastically, throwing weird ingredients together in ridiculously complicated meals. Emma was a great cook, Max remembered loyally. Meat and two veg, exactly what you wanted to eat, perfectly cooked. None of Allegra's nonsense.

Although there was something oddly endearing about the nonsense all the same. Even if it did taste rubbish.

'You say you want to be a serious journalist, but I've only ever seen you talk seriously about cosmetics or the latest soap,' he said, still puzzling over her.

A brisk wind was swirling dead leaves along the gutter and Allegra pulled her coat closer around her. 'People are more than one thing,' she said loftily. 'Talking of which, what did you do to Dickie?'

'I didn't do anything,' said Max in surprise.

'He was so fragile this morning that the entire office had to whisper! Stella's assistant told the intern who told me that when Stella asked him what was wrong, he said it was all your fault!'

'I just took him to the pub.'

Allegra had sent him off for another styling session with Dickie the night before. Max had grumbled, but he'd gone

along and without Allegra there had been able to come to
an understanding with Dickie. Make the whole process as
quick and painless as possible, he had suggested, and they
could go and have a decent drink.

'Can you believe it?' he went on. 'The guy's been in
London for ten years and he's never had a decent pint.'

'You took *Dickie* to a *pub?*' Allegra had stopped dead
and was looking at him in horror.

'You told me to be nice to him,' Max reminded her.

'Making him go to a pub and getting him drunk on
beer isn't being nice!'

'He had a great time. I'm taking him to a rugby game
next.'

Allegra opened and closed her mouth, unable to get out
a coherent sentence. 'Dickie…rugby…?'

'I don't know why you're all so terrified of him. He's
a perfectly nice guy once you get past all the affectation.'

'That's it. My career is over.'

'Don't be silly,' said Max, taking her arm and steering
her across the road at the lights. 'Dickie likes me. Although
if I'd thought about it, ending your career might have been
a good move. I'd never have to waltz again.'

'Darcy's going to be here any minute. Are you almost
ready?'

Allegra put her head around the door to the kitchen,
where Max was putting the final garnish to the romantic
vegetarian meal for two that they had planned together.

At least, she had planned it and Max had reluctantly
agreed to cook it. 'I don't see why I can't just give her
pasta with a tomato sauce,' he'd grumbled.

'Because this is a special occasion. You want Darcy to
know that you've made a real effort to cook something
that she'll really like.'

Eventually they had settled on a pear, walnut and gorgonzola salad to start, followed by mushroom strudels with a tarragon cream sauce, and then margarita ice cream with chocolate-dipped strawberries. Allegra had been pleased with it, but after several practice runs, she had strudel coming out of her ears and she couldn't face another chocolate-dipped strawberry, which wasn't something she ever thought she would say.

'I'm all set,' said Max. 'I just need to change.'

'I'll make the living room look nice,' Allegra volunteered. Max was supposed to be thinking about that as well, but when she had suggested it he had just looked blank.

At least everything was tidy, the way it always was when Max was around. Allegra set out candles and plumped up the cushions before putting on the playlist of romantic music she had compiled specially. Max didn't have a clue about music or romance, so she'd known better than to suggest that he did it.

She was lighting candles when he came back. 'It's a bit gloomy in here, isn't it?' he said, looking around. 'Darcy won't be able to see what she's eating.'

'It's not gloomy. It's *romantic.*'

Allegra straightened from the candles and studied Max, who had replaced his checked shirt with one in a dark mulberry colour that shrieked expensive and stylish. He was wearing new black jeans too, and all in all he was looking mighty fine. So fine, in fact, that she forgot about the match burning in her hand.

'Ouch!' Allegra shook the match from her hand and sucked her finger. 'Is that the shirt Dickie picked out for you?' she asked, covering her sudden confusion by bending to pick up the match.

'Of course.' Max plucked at it in distaste. 'You wouldn't catch me buying a red shirt, but Dickie insisted.'

'He was right. You look good,' said Allegra honestly. She tossed the blackened match into the bin and turned back to face him. She had herself back under control. 'If I could just make one teeny change…?'

Without waiting for Max to agree, she walked over and undid another button at his throat. Ignoring his protests, she turned her attention to his cuffs, unfastening them and rolling them up above his wrists.

But standing so close to him was making her feel a bit light-headed, and she was excruciatingly conscious of her fingertips grazing his forearms with their fine, flat hairs. The air had shortened, making her heart pound ridiculously. She wanted to say something light, something casual to break the atmosphere, but her mind was a blank and she didn't dare meet Max's eyes in case…

In case *what?*

In case he kissed her. In case *she* kissed *him*.

Allegra swallowed hard. This was silly. She'd just got over that mad period when she'd been so inexplicably conscious of him. The last few days had been fine, cooking, talking easily, sniping at each other, laughing with each other. They'd dutifully practised the basic waltz step and even seemed to be getting the hang of it. It had been just like the old days.

And now he'd put on a new shirt and that awful thump was back in her belly. Allegra didn't like it one little bit.

Clearing her throat, she patted the second sleeve into place and stepped back. 'There, that's better,' she said.

Max immediately started fidgeting with his cuffs. 'It looks so messy like this,' he complained until Allegra had to slap his hands away.

'Leave them! Those cuffs are the difference between looking like a nerd and looking like a hunk.'

'A *hunk?*' Max echoed, revolted.

'Okay, not a hunk,' she amended, 'but more normal, anyway. Like you might possibly have some social skills. And, talking of which,' she said as she struck another match to light the rest of the candles, 'remember this evening's about making Darcy feel really special. Ask her lots of questions about what she does and how she feels about things.'

'Yeah, yeah, we've been through this,' said Max, straightening the knives and forks on the table.

Allegra blew out the match and admired the way the flames danced above the candles. 'Are you sure it's all under control in the kitchen?'

'Positive. I wrote out a time plan, and I don't need to do anything until seventeen minutes after she arrives.'

'Right. Seventeen minutes. Because you wouldn't want to eat a minute later than scheduled, would you?' Allegra rolled her eyes, but Max was unfazed.

'You're the one who wants the meal to be a success,' he pointed out. He looked at his watch yet again. 'Shouldn't she be here by now?'

'I sent a car. I hope she's not going to be late. We can't really have a drink until she gets here, and I'm gasping for one.'

'We could practice our waltz steps,' Max suggested without any enthusiasm, but Allegra jumped up.

'That's a great idea. We need to be able to wow Cathy with our progress next week.'

They had practised several times now and it no longer felt uncomfortable to rest one hand on his shoulder, or to feel his arm around her waist. They set off briskly, moving their feet around an invisible box, the way Cathy had taught them, while Allegra hummed an approximation of a waltz.

'Hey, we're getting good at this,' Max said after a while. 'Shall we try a turn?'

Allegra was up for it but, the moment they tried to do something different, their feet got muddled up and they stumbled. Disentangling themselves, they tried again. This time they managed so well that Max got fancy. They were both elated at their success and, laughing, he spun her round and dipped her over his arm with a flourish.

And there it would have ended if they hadn't made the mistake of looking into each other's eyes. They could have straightened, still laughing, and it would have been fine.

But no! Their eyes had to lock so that the laughter evaporated without warning, leaving their smiles to fade. Allegra was still bent ridiculously over Max's arm but she couldn't tear her gaze from his. The air felt as if it was tightening around them, squeezing out all the oxygen, and her pulse was booming and thudding. She couldn't have moved if she had tried.

Later, she wondered if she had imagined the fact that Max's head had started to move down to hers. Certainly at the time she didn't know whether to be relieved or disappointed when the shrill of the doorbell jerked them both out of their daze.

'Darcy!' Flustered, Allegra pulled out of Max's hold and smoothed down her hair. What was she *doing*? She had forgotten all about the article for a few moments there.

Allegra had forgotten quite how beautiful Darcy was. Max greeted her at the door and when he showed her in she seemed to light up the room. Her blonde hair fell over one shoulder in a fishtail braid that looked casual but must have taken her hours to achieve, and her skin glowed. She was wearing an electric-blue dress that showed off her stupendous figure. If Allegra wasn't much mistaken, the dress was from a high street chain rather than a designer but Darcy made it look stunning. From her bee-stung lips to the tips of her Christian Louboutin shoes—no whiff of the high street *there*—she was perfect.

By rights, Allegra ought to hate her, but Darcy was so warm and friendly that it was impossible.

'This all looks wonderful,' she said, looking around the room. 'You've gone to so much trouble, Max!'

Max took it without a blink. 'Nothing's too much trouble for you, Darcy,' he said, but he avoided Allegra's eyes. 'Now, let's have some champagne...'

Everything was going swimmingly, Allegra thought later. Dom turned up a few minutes later and took a few pictures of Max in the kitchen, and then of Max and Darcy sitting at the table with the starter, but once he had gone they were able to enjoy the meal. The three of them chatted so easily that Allegra kept forgetting that she was supposed to be just an observer, and after a while she put her notebook aside.

She had imagined that taut moment of awareness just before Darcy rang the doorbell, she told herself. Look at them now, talking like old friends. There was no crackling in the air between them, no zing every time their eyes met. She had made the whole thing up.

The food wasn't too bad either. What it lacked in presentational flair, it made up for in efficiency, with Max putting each course on the table with military precision.

All in all, the second task was a huge success, Allegra congratulated herself.

'Coffee?' Max asked at last.

'Actually, I'd love a herbal tea if you've got one,' said Darcy, and Max rolled an agonized look at Allegra.

'In the cupboard above the kettle,' she said.

The moment Max went out to put the kettle on, Darcy leant towards Allegra. 'Can I ask you something?'

'Sure,' said Allegra in surprise.

'Are you guys...?'

'What?'

'You and Max,' said Darcy delicately. 'I asked Max if you were an item, but he said you were just friends.' She looked at Allegra. 'Is that right?'

Allegra felt unaccountably miffed at the way Max had disclaimed any interest in her, but she could hardly deny it. 'Of course,' she said, taking a casual sip of wine. 'Max is practically my brother.'

'Oh, that's good. So you won't mind if I asked Max to dinner at my place?'

Allegra choked on her wine. 'Dinner?' she spluttered.

'Yes. Not as part of the *Glitz* deal, but like a proper date.'

'You want to date *Max*?'

Darcy laughed a little self-consciously. 'I think he's cute.'

Max? *Cute*?

'He's not like the usual guys I date,' Darcy went on.

Allegra thought of the actors and rock stars who had been linked to Darcy, über hunks every one of them, and she blinked. 'You can say that again.'

'I kinda like him,' Darcy confessed. 'Do you think he'd say yes?'

A famous lingerie model inviting him to spend the evening alone with her at her house. Like Max would turn *that* invitation down.

'You should ask Max, not me,' said Allegra stiffly.

'You don't sound very keen on the idea,' said Darcy, who was a lot more perceptive than she looked. 'Are you sure you don't mind?'

'It's not that. It's just…well, Max puts on a good show, but his fiancée broke off their engagement not very long ago. I wouldn't want him to get hurt again. I mean…'

Allegra was floundering, wishing she had never started on this. '…It's just that you're so gorgeous and you must have so many men after you. I…I'd hate it if you were just amusing yourself with Max and he ended up taking you too seriously. And I can see why he would,' she said with honest envy. 'I can't imagine any guy not falling heavily for you.'

'You'd be surprised,' said Darcy with a touch of bitterness. 'I don't understand why I've got such a reputation as a man-eater. Nobody ever worries that I might be the one to get hurt, do they?'

'Max isn't your usual type,' Allegra pointed out and Darcy nodded.

'That's why I'd like to get to know him better. I'm sick of guys who are all moody and dramatic, or who just want to be with me so they can get their name in the papers.'

'Well, you certainly wouldn't need to worry about that with Max.'

'Great. Well, if you're sure you're okay with it, I'll ask him.'

Allegra wasn't at all sure that she *was* okay with it, but she couldn't think of a single reason why not. Max was a grown man. He didn't need her to look after him, and she could hardly veto his chance to fulfil every man's fantasy of going out with Darcy, could she? He deserved some fun after Emma's rejection.

So why did she have this leaden feeling in her stomach?

When Max came back with the coffee and the herbal tea, Allegra took her mug and excused herself. 'I'll leave you two together,' she said with a brilliant smile. 'I need to go and write up my notes. Have fun.'

* * *

'What do you mean, you're not coming?' Max stared at Allegra in consternation.

'I'm going to dinner at Flick's,' she pointed out. 'Plus, I'm not invited.'

'I thought you'd be going too. And Dom.'

'Max, Darcy's invited you to supper. It's nothing to do with the article.'

'Why?' he asked, puzzled.

'Crazy thought, but maybe she likes you.'

Thrown by this new information, Max dragged a hand through his hair. The truth was that he hadn't really listened when Darcy had invited him the evening he'd cooked her dinner. It was after Allegra had gone to her room, and he'd just assumed that another task was involved.

Darcy *liked* him?

'You mean, like on a date?' he asked cautiously and Allegra rolled her eyes. She was doing something complicated with her hair in front of the mirror over the mantelpiece.

'I'd have thought you'd have been over the moon,' she said, through a mouthful of hairclips.

'Darcy King wants to go out with *me*?'

'I know, I thought it was unlikely too,' said Allegra, fixing another clip into place.

Max sat on the sofa and tossed the remote from hand to hand. Darcy King. She was gorgeous, sexy, warm, *nice*. Why wasn't he ecstatic?

'I thought I was just signing up for this article of yours,' he said grouchily. 'I didn't realise I'd be getting involved in other stuff as well.'

'It's just dinner, Max. I don't suppose she's planning on a bout of eye-popping sex straight away.'

Apparently satisfied with her hair, Allegra turned from

the mirror. It never failed to amaze Max how she could spend so long achieving a range of hairstyles, each messier than the last. That evening she had twisted it up and fixed it into place with a clip, but bits stuck out wildly from the clip, and other strands fell around her face. Max's fingers itched to smooth them behind her ears, but the idea of sliding his fingers through that silky hair was so tantalising that for a moment he lost track of the conversation.

'You ought to be flattered,' she said.

'I am,' said Max, wrenching his mind back from a disturbingly vivid image of pulling that clip from her hair and letting it fall, soft and shiny, to her shoulders. 'It's just...I don't want to complicate things.'

'What's complicated about dinner? You had dinner with Darcy the other night and this time you won't even have to worry about the cooking.'

'It's not that.' How could he tell Allegra that, much as he liked Darcy, he found her a bit overwhelming? 'It's not long since I was engaged to Emma,' he said, grasping at the excuse. 'It feels too soon to be getting involved with anyone else.'

Allegra's face softened instantly and then she snarled every one of his senses by coming to sit on the sofa beside him and placing her hand on his knee.

'I'm sorry, I keep forgetting that you must still be gutted about Emma.'

Max didn't think gutted was quite the right word, in fact, but with Allegra sitting so close, her green eyes huge and warm with sympathy, it was all he could do to nod.

'Darcy knows you were engaged,' Allegra went on, with a comforting rub on his thigh. At least, Max assumed it was meant to be comforting, although in practice it was excruciatingly arousing. If she moved her hand any higher, he couldn't be responsible for his actions… As unobtrusively as he could, he shifted along the sofa.

Allegra was still talking, still looking at him with those big, earnest eyes, completely unaware of the effect she was having on him. 'She won't expect you to fall madly in love with her, Max. It'll just be dinner. Darcy's nice, and it'll be a boost for your ego, if nothing else. You should go and forget about Emma for an evening.'

It wasn't Emma he needed to forget, it was the feel of Allegra's hand on his leg, but Max heard himself agreeing just so that he could get up before he grabbed her and rolled her beneath him on the sofa. He had to give himself a few mental slaps before he had himself under control enough to change and go back down to the sitting room, where Allegra was perched on the armchair and bending over to ease on a pair of precipitously-heeled shoes. She was in a dark floral sleeveless dress with black lace over the shoulders and a skirt that showed off miles of leg in black stockings, and Max's throat promptly dried all over again.

Those loose strands of hair had slithered forward when she bent her head and she tucked them behind her ears as she glanced up to see Max standing in the doorway. There was an odd little jump in the air as their eyes met, and then both looked away.

'You look nice,' Max said gruffly.

'Thank you.' Her gaze skimmed his then skittered away. 'Is that one of the shirts Dickie picked out for you?'

'Yes.' Self-consciously, he held his arms out from his side. 'Why, is it too casual?'

'It's perfect—or it would be if you rolled up your cuffs, and…' Allegra pointed at her throat to indicate that his collar was too tightly buttoned.

She had a thing about his collar, but Max knew from experience that it wasn't worth the argument. With a long-suffering sigh, he unfastened another button before starting on his cuffs. She had a thing about those too. He could do them up again as soon as she'd gone.

'So, you're seeing your mother,' he said after a moment. 'What's it going to be? A cosy night in with just the two of you?'

Max knew as well as she did that Flick didn't do cosy, but Allegra couldn't help smiling a little wistfully. She adored her mother, and it made her feel disloyal to wish sometimes that Flick could be a little—just a little!—more like Libby and Max's mum, who was easygoing and gave wonderful hugs and would happily watch *I'm a Celebrity Get Me Out of Here!* instead of the news. The first time Allegra had been to stay with Libby they had had supper on their laps in front of the television, and it had felt deliciously subversive.

'I think there'll be a few people there,' she told Max as she wiggled her feet into a more comfortable position in her shoes. 'She says she's got someone she wants me to meet.'

Max started on his second cuff, his expression sardonic. 'Flick's setting you up with a new boyfriend?'

'Maybe.'

'You don't sound very keen.'

She hadn't, had she? She'd sounded like someone who would really rather be staying at home. That would never do.

Allegra stood up and tested her shoes. 'Of course I'm keen,' she said. 'The men my mother introduces me to are always intelligent, cultured, amusing, interesting... Why wouldn't I be keen?'

'No reason when you put it like that,' said Max. He had dealt with his cuffs and now he stood in the centre of the room with his hands in his pockets, looking sulky and surly and disconcertingly attractive. Allegra almost told him to button up his shirt again so he could go back to looking stuffy and repressed.

'I'm feeling positive,' she said airily. 'This guy could be The One. I could be on my way to meet true love!'

Max snorted. 'Well, don't make a date for Wednesday, that's all.'

He had finally heard from Bob Laskovski's office. Bob and his wife would be in London the following week and the dinner to meet Max and his 'fiancée' was arranged for the Wednesday night. Max was nervous about the whole business, Allegra knew. He wasn't comfortable with deception, but he was desperate for the Shofrar job. Perhaps that was why he was so grouchy at the moment?

Darcy was welcome to him, Allegra told herself as she flipped open her phone to call a cab. She couldn't care less that Max was having supper with a lingerie model. *She* was going out to have a great time and meet a fabulous new guy. And, who knew, maybe she'd find true love at last as well.

Flick still lived in the four-storey Georgian house in a much sought after part of Islington where Allegra had grown up but it never felt like going home. The house was immaculately decorated and most visitors gasped in envy when they stepped inside, but Allegra much preferred the Warriners' house with its scuffed skirting boards and faded chair covers.

Flick's dinner parties were famous, less for the food, which was always catered, than for the company. Politicians, media stars, business leaders, diplomats, writers, artists, musicians, journalists…anyone who was anyone in London jostled for a coveted invitation to sit at Flick's dining table. No celebrities, pop stars or soap opera actors need apply, though. Flick insisted on a certain intellectual rigour.

Thus Allegra found herself sitting between Dan, a fast-track civil servant, obviously destined for greatness, while William, on her right, was a political aide. They both worked in government circles and were both high-flyers, full of gossip and opinion.

Toying with her marinated scallops, Allegra felt boring and uninformed in comparison. She couldn't think of a single clever or witty thing to say.

Not that it mattered much. The conversation around the table was fast and furious as usual, but no one was interested in her opinion anyway, and it was enough for Allegra to keep a smile fixed to her face.

Beside her, Dan had launched into a scurrilous story about a politician everybody else seemed to know but who Allegra had never heard of. She laughed when everybody else laughed, but she was wondering how Max was getting on with Darcy. Would he sleep with her? Allegra realised that she had stopped smiling and hurriedly put her smile back in place.

Why did she care? Max would be leaving soon anyway, and it wasn't as if he was interested in her. True, there had been that moment when their eyes had met earlier, when she was putting on her shoes and had glanced up to find him watching her and something had leapt in the air between them.

It was just because they were spending so much time together for the article, Allegra told herself. It wasn't that she would really rather be sharing pizza with Max in front of the television than sitting here at this glamorous, glittering party. Of course she wouldn't.

Oh, God, she had missed Dan's punchline. At the other

end of the table, she caught Flick's eye and the tiny admonishing frown and sat up straighter.

Beside her, William was filling her glass, teasing her out of her abstraction. His eyes were warm, and she was picking up definite vibes. Allegra gazed at him, determined to find him attractive. She'd already established that he'd split up with his long-term girlfriend a year ago. A mutual thing, he'd said. They were still friends.

So no obvious emotional baggage. Unlike Max, who was still sore about Emma.

William was very good-looking. Charming. Assured. Also unlike Max.

He would be staying in London. Unlike Max.

He seemed to be finding her attractive. Unlike Max.

He was perfect boyfriend material. Unlike Max.

If William asked her out, she would say yes.

Definitely. She might even fall in love with him.

CHAPTER SIX

'I HAVEN'T HAD a chance to talk to you yet, Allegra,' Flick said, coming back into the dining room, having said good-bye to the last of her guests, a cabinet minister who was tipped for a promotion in the next reshuffle. She frowned at Allegra, who was helping the caterers to clear the table. 'The caterers are paid to tidy up. Leave that and let's have a chat.'

No one looking at them together would guess that they were mother and daughter. Where Allegra was tall and dark and a little quirky-looking, Flick was petite and blonde with perfect features, steely blue eyes and a ferocious intelligence. Allegra was super-proud of her famous mother, but sometimes she did wonder what it would be like to have a mother who would rush out to hug you when you arrived, like Libby and Max's mother did, or fuss over you if you were unhappy.

A chat with Flick didn't mean sitting over cocoa in the kitchen. It meant being interrogated in the study about your career and achievements. Which in Allegra's case were not very many.

Sure enough, Flick led the way to her book-lined study and sat behind her desk, gesturing Allegra to a chair as if for an interview.

'Another successful evening, I think,' she said complacently.

'The food was lovely,' Allegra said dutifully, stealing a surreptitious glance at her watch. One in the morning... Was Max still with Darcy? He'd seemed surprisingly reluctant to go, but surely, once faced with Darcy's glowing beauty, he wouldn't be able to resist?

'You seem very abstracted, Allegra.' Flick had her razor-sharp interviewing voice on. 'I noticed it during dinner too. Not very good manners. Would you rather go?'

'No, no, of course not...' Nobody could make her stammer like her mother and, because she knew it irritated Flick, Allegra pulled herself together. 'I'm sorry. I'm just a bit preoccupied with an assignment I've got for *Glitz*.'

Flick sat back in her chair and raised her brows. 'I hardly think an article on the latest fashion trend compares to the kind of issues that everyone else here has to deal with every day.' She unbent a little. 'But I read your little piece on shoes last week. It was very entertaining. The ending was a little weak but, otherwise, your writing has improved considerably. What's the latest assignment?'

Allegra started to explain about the idea behind the article, but it sounded stupid when her mother was listening with her impeccably groomed head on one side. 'I'm hoping that if I can make a success of it, Stella will give me more opportunities to write something different.' She stumbled to a halt at last.

Flick nodded her approval. She liked it when Allegra thought strategically. 'I suppose it's experience of a sort, but you'd be so much better off at a serious magazine. You remember Louise's son, Joe? He's at *The Economist* now.'

Allegra set her teeth. 'I'm not sure I'm ready to write about quantitative easing yet, Flick. *The Economist* would be a bit of a leap from *Glitz*.'

'Not for someone who's got what it takes—but you've never been ambitious,' said Flick regretfully. 'But you do look very nice tonight,' she conceded. 'Those dark florals are good for you. The earrings aren't quite right, but otherwise, yes, very nice. William seemed rather taken,' she added. 'Are you going to see him again?'

'Perhaps.' The truth was that when William had asked her out, Allegra had opened her mouth to say yes and then somehow heard herself say that she was rather busy at the moment.

'He's got a great future ahead of him. I'd like to see you spend more time with people like that instead of these silly little assignments for that magazine. I mean, who are you working with at the moment?'

'Max.' Funny how his name felt awkward in her mouth now. 'You remember, Libby's brother,' she said when Flick looked blank.

'Oh, yes…rather dull.'

'He isn't dull!' Allegra flushed angrily.

'I don't remember him striking me as very interesting,' said Flick, dismissive as only she could be.

Allegra had a clear memory of thinking much the same thing once. So why was she wishing that she could have spent the evening with him instead of flirting with William, who was everything Max would never be?

'I didn't realise he was a particular friend of yours.' Her mother's eyes had narrowed suspiciously at the colour burning in Allegra's cheeks.

'He wasn't. I mean, he isn't. He's just living in the house for a couple of months while Libby's in Paris.'

'I hope you're not getting involved with him?'

'Anyone would think he was some kind of trouble-maker,' Allegra grumbled. 'He's a civil engineer. It doesn't get more respectable than that.'

'I'm sure he's very good at what he does,' said Flick
gently. 'But he's not exactly a mover and shaker, is he?
I've always worried about the way you seem happy to
settle for the mediocre, rather than fulfilling your potential.' She shook her head. 'I blame myself for letting
you spend so much time with that family—what are they
called? Warren?'

'Warriner,' said Allegra, 'and they're wonderful.'

'Oh, I'm sure they're very kind but I've brought you up
to aim for the exceptional.'

'They *are* exceptional!' Normally the thinning of Flick's
lips would have been a warning to Allegra, but she was
too angry to stop there. 'They're exceptionally generous
and exceptionally fun. Max's mother might not win any
style awards, but she's lovely, and his dad is one of the nic-
est, most decent, most honourable men I've ever met,' she
swept on. 'I only wish I'd had a father like him!'

There was a moment of appalled silence, while her last
words rang around the room. Flick had whitened. Allegra's
lack of a father was a taboo subject and Allegra knew it.

'I'm sorry,' she said, letting out a long breath. 'But why
won't you tell me about my father?'

'I don't wish to discuss it,' said Flick tightly. 'In your
case, father is a biological term and nothing more. I'm
sorry if I haven't been enough of a parent for you.'

'I didn't mean that,' Allegra tried to break in wretch-
edly, but Flick moved smoothly on.

'I can only assure you that all I've ever wanted is the
best for you. You have so much potential if only you would
realise it. I really think it would be a mistake for you to
tie yourself down to somebody ordinary who'll just drag
you down to his level.'

She should have known better than to try and press
Flick about her father. 'You don't need to worry,' said

Allegra dully. 'There's no question of anything between Max and me and, even if there were, he's going abroad to work soon.'

'Just as well,' said Flick.

It *was* just as well, Allegra told herself in the taxi home. Flick had suggested that she stay the night in her old room, but she wanted to go back to the flat. She didn't want to admit to herself that she needed to know if Max had stayed with Darcy or not and it was like a sword being drawn out of her entrails when she opened the door and saw Max stretched out on the sofa.

'You're back early.' Funny, her voice sounded light and normal when her heart was behaving so oddly, racing and lurching, bouncing off her chest wall like a drunk.

'It's half past one. It's not that early.'

'I suppose not.' Allegra went to sit in the armchair. She picked at the piping. 'So, how was your evening?'

'Fine. Yours?'

'Oh, you know. Lots of clever, glamorous guests. Witty conversation. Delicious food. The usual.'

'Your average social nightmare.'

Allegra laughed and toed off her shoes so that she could curl her feet up beneath her. She was feeling better already.

'So, did you find your true love over the canapés?' Max asked.

'I don't know about that,' she said. 'I sat between two handsome, ambitious single men specially picked out for me by my mother.'

Max's gaze flickered to her face and then away. 'So who's the lucky guy?'

'Neither.' Reaching up, she pulled the clips from her hair and shook it loose, oblivious to the way Max's eyes darkened. 'I've decided I need a relationship detox. I might abstain from all men for a while.'

'That would be a shame.'

'I'm sick of feeling that they only ask me out be-cause I'm Flick Fielding's daughter.' It was the first time Allegra had said it out loud and she winced as she heard the resentment reverberating around the room.

'That's not why they ask you out,' said Max roughly.

'Isn't it? Why else would they? I'm not clever the way they are. I can't contribute to the conversation. I've got nothing to offer.'

'You're beautiful,' said Max. 'Come on, Legs, you must know you are,' he said when she gaped at him. 'You're gor-geous. Any man would be glad to be seen with you. I don't know who you sat next to tonight, but if you think he was more interested in Flick's influence than in the way you looked, you're not thinking straight!'

He would have been the one not thinking straight if he'd been sitting next to Allegra while she was wearing that dress. He would have been mesmerised by her arms, bare and slender, by those expressive hands, by the glow of her skin and the way the straight shiny hair threatened to slip out of its clips. He would have spent his whole time imagining how it would look falling to her shoulders, the way it was now.

He wouldn't have been able to eat, Max knew. His mouth would have been too dry and he'd have been too busy watching the sweep of her lashes, the brightness of her eyes, the tempting hollow of her cleavage, the curve of her breasts... And thinking about her bare knees under the table, the long, sexy legs in those ridiculous shoes.

His head felt light and he realised it was because he'd stopped breathing. Max sucked in a steadying breath. Where had all that come from?

'I didn't know you thought I was beautiful,' said Allegra, sounding thrown.

'I thought so many other people would tell you there was no need for me to do the same. You're still deeply irritating, mind,' he said in an effort to drag the conversation back onto safe ground, 'but of course you're beautiful. I thought you knew.'

'No.' Allegra bent her head, pushing back the hair that slithered forward, but he still couldn't see her face properly.

It was probably just as well. Max was uneasily aware that something tenuous had insinuated itself into the air, like a memory hovering just out of reach, or a forgotten word trembling on the tip of a tongue. Something that seemed to be drawing the air tighter, squeezing out the oxygen so that his chest felt tight and his breathing oddly sticky.

Could Allegra feel it?

Apparently not. Even as he struggled to heave in another breath, she was lifting her head and focusing on him with those eyes that seemed to get more beautiful every time he looked into them.

'Tell me how you got on with Darcy,' she said, sounding so completely normal that Max squirmed inwardly with humiliation. *She* wasn't finding it hard to breathe. She wasn't aware of the tension in the air, or snarled in a knot of inconvenient and inappropriate lust.

'I wondered if you'd end up staying the night,' she went on, but not as if she cared one way or the other.

So he obviously couldn't admit that she was the reason he wasn't tucked up next to the world's favourite lingerie model right now.

Because Darcy had made it very clear that she was up for a lot more than just dinner, but it hadn't felt right, not when he'd spent most of the evening wondering what Allegra was doing and who her bloody mother had lined up to sit next to her. Flick might be keen on big brains, but

Max was prepared to bet that they were men too, and that they wouldn't be above a flirtatious touch every now and then: Allegra's shoulder, her hand, her knee...

It was only when Darcy had looked at him strangely that he'd realised he was grinding his teeth.

What was wrong with him? Max had wanted to tear out his hair. There he was, sitting across the table from *Darcy King*, with a clear invitation to get his hands on that luscious body. It was the opportunity of a lifetime, a fantasy come true for a million men like him, and all he could think about was his sister's scrawny friend! He had to be sickening for something. Or certifiable.

Or both.

He liked Darcy, he really did, but it had been awkward. He told Allegra what he'd told Darcy, which was the best excuse he could come up with at the time.

'I don't really want to get involved with Darcy,' he said. 'She's nice but...well, I don't see her fitting into my life, do you? I can't imagine someone like Darcy out in Shofrar, and I don't feel like being just a novelty plaything for her. I know most other men would give their eye teeth to be toyed with by her, but I'm not sure it would be worth it.'

It wasn't really an excuse. It was *true*. Not that Allegra seemed to be convinced.

She looked at him strangely. 'I doubt that Darcy's thinking about anything serious,' she said. 'It would only be a bit of fun. Where does Shofrar come into it?'

'That's where my life is going to be,' said Max stiffly, even as he winced inwardly at what a pompous jerk he sounded. But the words kept coming out of his mouth without taking the trouble of detouring through his brain. 'There's no point in getting involved with someone who can't hack it away from a city.'

Meaning *what* exactly? He wasn't surprised at the way Allegra's face clouded with disbelief.

'So, let me get this right. You're saying that you're not going to have sex unless you can get married to someone who won't mind being dragged out to some desert hell-hole so that she can play second fiddle to your career?'

'Yes...no!' What *was* he saying?

'Isn't that going to be a bit limiting?'

Max was beginning to sweat. He hadn't felt this out of control since Emma had blithely broken off their engagement.

Emma! He grabbed onto the thought of his fiancée. *Ex*-fiancée. 'Look, I'm not the sort of guy who goes out with models,' he said with a tinge of desperation. 'In a fantasy, maybe, but I really just want to be with someone like Emma. I think being with Darcy made me realise that I wasn't really over Emma yet.'

Which might even be true. Not the realisation, which in reality hadn't crossed his mind at the time, but that he was still missing Emma at some level.

Now that he thought about it, Max thought it probably was true. It would explain the muddle inside him, wouldn't it? Max *hated* feeling like this, as if he were churning around in some massive washing machine, not knowing which way was up. Not knowing what he thought or what he felt. He hadn't felt himself since Emma had wafted off in search of passion.

'I sent Emma a text, just like you suggested,' he told Allegra almost accusingly, and she sat up straighter.

'Did she reply?'

'While I was on my way to Darcy's. So I was thinking about her before I got there.'

That *was* true, although he hadn't really been thinking about Emma in a yearning way, more in a how-odd-I-don't-really-feel-anything-when-I-see-your-name-now kind of way. Until a week or so ago, Max would have said that all he wanted was to hear from Emma and try to get back to normal again, but when he'd read her text he hadn't felt the rush of relief and hope that he'd expected.

At least Allegra was looking sympathetic now. 'I can see that would throw you a bit,' she said fairly. 'What did Emma say?'

'Nothing really. Just that she was fine and how was I?'

'Oh, that's very encouraging!' Allegra beamed at him and he looked back suspiciously.

'It is?'

'Definitely. If Emma didn't want to stay in contact, she wouldn't have replied at all. As it is, she not only responded, she asked you a question back.'

'So?'

'So she's opening a dialogue,' Allegra said with heavy patience. 'She's asked how you are, which means you reply and tell her, and say something else, then she gets the chance to react to that... Before you know where you are, you're having a conversation, and then it's only a matter of time before you decide you should meet.'

She sat back, satisfied with her scenario. 'It's a really good sign, Max,' she assured him. 'I bet Emma's bored with her passionate guy already and was thrilled to hear from you.'

Max couldn't see it. *Thrilled*. There was an Allegra word for you. Emma wasn't the kind of woman who was *thrilled* about things. It was one of the things he had always liked about her. Emma didn't make a big fuss about anything. She was moderation, balance, calm—unlike some people he could mention.

He looked at Allegra, who was curled up in the arm-chair, bright-eyed and a little tousled at the end of the evening, apparently unaware that her dress was rucked up, exposing a mouth-watering length of leg. When he thought about Allegra, he didn't think moderation. He thought extravagance. Allegra dealt in extremes. She *adored* things or she *loathed* them. She was wildly excited at the prospect of something or dreading it. She was madly in love or broken-hearted. It was exhausting trying to keep up with the way her emotions swung around. Emma had never left his head reeling.

Of course, Emma was the one who had thrown up her nice, safe life for a passionate affair, so what did he know?

Max hunched his shoulders morosely. Women. Just when you thought you understood them, they turned around and kicked your legs out from beneath you, leaving you floundering.

Look at Allegra, who had just been Libby's mildly annoying friend. He'd known exactly where he was with her. True, there had been that odd little moment a few years ago but, apart from that, it had been an easy relationship. Nothing about her seemed easy now. He couldn't look at her without noticing her skin or the silkiness of her hair. Without thinking about her legs or her mouth or the tantalising hollow of her throat.

Without blurting out that she looked beautiful.

Max didn't know exactly what Allegra had done to change, but she had done *something*.

Now she was fiddling with her hair, smoothing it behind her ear, grooming herself like a cat. 'So have you replied to her?' she asked.

'What?' Mesmerised by her fingers, Max had forgotten what she was talking about.

Allegra looked at him. 'Have you replied to Emma?' she repeated slowly, and Max felt a dull colour burning along his cheekbones.

'Oh. No, not yet.'

'You're playing it cool?'

Max was damned if he knew.

What if Allegra was right? What if Emma really was waiting to hear from him? If they could miraculously make everything right, get married as planned, and go out to Shofrar? He ought to feel happy at the idea…oughtn't he? But all he really felt was confused.

He met Allegra's expectant gaze. Playing it cool sounded a lot better than not having a clue what was going on.

'Something like that,' he said.

'Allegra!' Max banged his fist on the bathroom door. 'What in God's name are you doing in there?'

'Nearly ready,' Allegra called back. Carefully, she smoothed her lipstick into place and blotted her mouth. She wouldn't for the world admit it to Max, but she was nervous about the evening ahead. This dinner with Bob Laskovski and his wife was so important to him. She didn't want to let him down.

Max had been in a funny mood for the last few days. Allegra had decided that hearing from Emma had thrown him more than he understood. He was in denial, but it was obvious that he really wanted Emma back. Why else would he resist Darcy?

It had been easier to go out and leave him to be morose on his own, and when William got in touch after dinner at Flick's she had agreed to meet him for a drink after all. The whole relationship detox thing would never have worked anyway, Allegra decided. She should at least give him a chance.

William was good company, good-looking, and she enjoyed herself, and she wouldn't let herself think that looking at William's patrician mouth didn't make her stomach hurt the way it did when she looked at Max's.

Because there was no point in thinking about Max that way.

Allegra couldn't even explain what kind of way that was, but it was something to do with a trembly sensation just below her skin, with a thudding in her veins that started whenever Max came into the room. It was something to do with the way every sense seemed on full alert when he was near.

Being so aware of him the whole time made her uncomfortable. It was crazy. It was inappropriate. It didn't make sense.

It was just the assignment, she tried to reassure herself. It was just spending so much time with him. It wasn't *real*. A temporary madness, that was all. Max would go to Shofrar and she would go back to normal.

She couldn't wait.

Max had been very clear. He wasn't interested in a quick fling. He was looking for someone who could be part of his life, someone who would share his interests and not mind being dragged around the world. It wasn't Darcy, and it sure as hell wasn't her either, Allegra knew. She was the last kind of girl Max would ever want to get involved with…and the feeling was mutual, she hurried to remind herself whenever that thought seemed too depressing. It wasn't as if she wanted to leave London. She had a career here.

She might not be changing the world or writing groundbreaking articles, but she was doing what she wanted to do…wasn't she? Allegra's mind flickered to illustration then away. Drawing cartoon animals wasn't a serious job. She could do better for herself, as Flick was constantly telling her.

Besides, the article about Max was going to be her big break. She had already written the first half and it was pretty good, even if she did say so herself. Perhaps she was spending rather too much time sketching Max while she thought, but it was inevitable that she should be thinking about him. Right now, that was her job, that was all.

'*Allegra*! We're going to be late!' Max had just raised his fist to rap the bathroom door again when Allegra pulled it open. She smiled brightly at him, gratified by the way his jaw slackened.

'What do you think?' She pirouetted in the doorway. She was in the most demure outfit she could find, a killer LBD with a sheer décolletage and sleeves. Even Max couldn't object to a black dress, Allegra had reasoned, but she'd been unable to resist pimping up the plainness with glittery earrings and bling-studded stilettos. There was only so much plain dressing a girl could do, and she was counting on the fact that Max and his boss were men and therefore unlikely to even look at her shoes.

'Do I look sufficiently sensible?' she asked, and Max, who had evidently forgotten that his fist was still raised, lowered it slowly.

'Sensible isn't quite the word I was thinking of,' he said, sounding strained.

Allegra was disappointed. 'I've put my hair up and everything,' she protested. Her hair was so slippery it had taken ages to do, too.

'You look very nice,' Max said gruffly. 'Now, come on. The taxi's waiting. We need to get a move on.' His gaze travelled down her legs and ended at her shoes. 'Can you make it to the taxi?'

'Of course I can,' said Allegra, unsure whether to be pleased or miffed that he had noticed her shoes after all.

Her hair was precariously fixed, to say the least, so

Allegra settled back into the seat and pulled her seat belt on with care. She loved London taxis, loved their bulbous shape and the yellow light on top. She loved the smell of the seats, the clicking of the engine, the straps that stopped you sliding around on your seat when they turned a corner. Sitting in a taxi as it drove past the iconic London sights made Allegra feel as if she was at the centre of things, part of a great vibrant city. It gave her a thrill every time.

Every time except that night.

That night, the streets were a blur. Allegra couldn't concentrate on London. She was too aware of Max sitting beside her. He was sensibly strapped in too, and he wasn't touching her. He wasn't even close, but that didn't stop her whole side tingling as if the seat belt had vanished and she had slid across the seat to land against him.

She swallowed hard. This was so *silly*. She shouldn't have to make an effort to sound normal with Max.

'So,' she said brightly, 'what's the plan?'

'Plan?'

'We ought to get our stories straight about how we met at least.'

Max frowned. 'Bob's not going to be interested in that kind of thing.'

'His wife might be.'

It was obvious Max hadn't thought of that. 'Better stick to the truth,' he decided, and Allegra's brows rose.

'Won't that rather defeat the object of the exercise?'

'I don't mean about the pretence,' he said irritably. 'Just that I know you through my sister, that kind of thing.'

It all sounded a bit thin to Allegra, but Max clearly didn't think his boss was going to interrogate them in any detail. She just hoped that he was right.

'I don't think you'll have to do much but smile and

look as if we might conceivably be planning to get married,' Max said.

'How besotted do you want me to be?' she asked provocatively. It was easier needling him than noticing how the street lights threw the planes of his face into relief, how the passing headlights kept catching the corner of his mouth. 'I could be madly in love or just sweetly adoring.'

'Just be normal,' he said repressively. 'If you can.'

They were to meet Bob and his wife at Arturo's, a quiet and classic restaurant no longer at the forefront of fashion but still famous for its food. When they got there, Max paid off the taxi and ran a finger under his collar. He'd wanted to wear a plain white shirt but Allegra had bullied him into putting on the mulberry-coloured shirt Dickie had picked out for him, with a plain tie in a darker hue.

'Bob's going to wonder what the hell I'm doing in a red shirt,' he grumbled as he eased the collar away from his throat.

'Stop fiddling, you look great,' said Allegra. She stepped up and made his senses reel by straightening his tie and patting it into place. 'Really,' she told him, 'you look good. You just need to relax.'

'Relax, right,' said Max, taking refuge in sarcasm. 'I'm just going for the most important interview of my career so far, which means lying through my teeth to my new boss. What's there to feel tense about?'

'We don't have to lie if you don't want to. Why not just tell Bob the truth about Emma?'

For a moment Max was tempted. Wouldn't chucking in the towel be easier than spending the evening trying to convince Bob Laskovski that it was remotely credible that a girl like Allegra would choose to be with him? She was so clearly out of his league.

When she had opened the bathroom door and smiled at

him, it had been like a punch to his heart. 'Do I look sufficiently sensible?' she had asked while he was still struggling for breath, while he was trying to wrench his eyes off the way her dress clung enticingly to her slender body.

True, her arms and shoulders were covered but that sheer black stuff was somehow even more tantalising than bare skin would have been. It seemed to beckon him forward to peer closer, hinting at the creamy skin half hidden beneath the gauzy film of black. Between the sheer arms and shoulders and the tight-fitting dress, Max felt as if there were great neon arrows angled at her throat, at her breasts, at the curve of her hips: *Look here! Look here!*

The dress stopped above her knees—*Look here!* —revealing those killer legs of hers—*And here!*—ending in absurd shoes that were studded with mock jewels. Her earrings swung and glittered in the light and her hair, twisted up and back more neatly than usual, gleamed.

Once the oxygen had rushed back to his head, Max had been able to think of lots of words to describe Allegra right then: sexy, erotic, dazzling, gorgeous... Had he already mentioned sexy? But *sensible? Suitable?* Max didn't think so.

Now she was adjusting his tie and standing so close her perfume was coiling into his mind, and lust fisted in his belly. For a wild moment the need to touch her was so strong all Max could think about was grabbing her, pushing her up against a wall and putting his hands on her, touching her, feeling her, taking her.

Horrified by the urge, he took a step back. What was happening to him? He didn't do wild. He was sensible, steady, an engineer, not some macho type acting out his caveman fantasies.

Max shook his head slightly to clear it. This whole article business was getting to him, that was all. The sooner he got to Shofrar, the better. *That* was what he wanted, not to rip his little sister's friend's clothes off. And for Shofrar he needed Bob Laskovski's approval. Was he really going to risk blowing the project manager role he'd coveted for so long just because he was distracted by Allegra's perfume?

'No,' he said. His voice was a little hoarse, but firm. 'I want to stick with what we agreed.'

'Okay.' Allegra smiled at him and tucked her hand through his arm. 'In that case, let's go and get you that job, tiger.'

CHAPTER SEVEN

AT WORK, BOB LASKOVSKI was always referred to in hushed tones, and Max was expecting his boss to be an imposing figure. Headshots on the website showed a serious man with a shiny pate and a horseshoe of white hair but, in person, Bob was short and rotund with an easy smile and eyes that crinkled engagingly at the corners.

Max was relieved when Allegra let go of him so that he could shake hands with Bob, who turned to introduce his wife. No trophy wife for Bob: Karen Laskovski was silver-haired and very elegant. No doubt Allegra could have described what she was wearing in exhaustive detail, but Max just got an impression of warmth and charm and a light blue outfit.

And now it was his turn. Allegra smiled encouragingly when he glanced at her, and Max cleared his throat.

'This is my fiancée, Allegra.'

There, the lie was out. Max was sure he could hear it clanging around the restaurant and waited for the other diners to look up and shout *Liar! Liar!* but nobody seemed to notice anything unusual, least of all the Laskovskis. Couldn't they *see* what an ill-assorted couple he and Allegra were?

But no, apparently not.

'What a pretty name!' Karen exclaimed as Allegra beamed and shook hands.

'It means cheerful,' said Allegra.

'And you look like it's a good name for you,' said Bob, who had blinked a couple of times at Allegra's shoes.

Allegra smiled and, to Max's horror, she took hold of his arm once more and leant winsomely against his shoulder. 'I've got a lot to be cheerful about,' she said, fluttering her lashes at him. 'I'm just so excited to be marrying Max and going out to Shofrar with him. Hopefully,' she added, beaming a smile at Bob, who nodded approvingly.

'It's a great thing when you're both looking forward to a posting,' he said as he gestured for everyone to sit down. 'Especially a place like Shofrar, where there isn't much to occupy you if you're not working. Too often we see young engineers coming home early because their wife or partner isn't happy. But you're obviously going to be an ideal engineer's wife,' he said to Allegra.

Max covered his choke of disbelief with a cough. Hadn't Bob noticed Allegra's shoes? Couldn't he *see* that she was the last person who would be happy in the desert?

As for Allegra, she was well into her role. 'I don't mind where I am, as long as I'm with Max,' she said.

Forget journalism, she should have been an actress, thought Max, unaccountably ruffled. But Bob and Karen seemed to be lapping it up.

'It reminds me of when we were first married,' Karen said with a reminiscent smile at her husband. 'I didn't care as long as I could be with you.'

'Mind you, we were never really apart,' said Bob, covering her hand with his. 'We were high school sweethearts. I fell in love with Karen the moment I saw her, didn't I, honey?'

Max couldn't understand it. Bob was supposed to be

talking about contracts and deliverables, or quizzing Max on his project experience, not wittering on about love. Naturally, Allegra was encouraging him.

'Oh, that's so wonderful!' she cried, clapping her hands together. 'So you two believe in love at first sight?'

Max wanted to drop his head onto the table.

'We sure do,' said Bob with a fond glance at his wife, who gazed adoringly back at him. 'How about you two? You known each other a long time?'

'Years,' said Allegra, launching into an explanation of her friendship with Libby. 'For most of that time, Max and I ignored each other completely.'

'Aha!' Karen leaned forward. 'So what changed?'

For the first time, Allegra's cheery confidence faltered. 'I…well, I'm not sure…it just crept up on us, I guess.' And then she had the nerve to turn to *him*. 'What do you think, Max? When did you first realise that you were in love with me?'

It was as if the restaurant had jarred to a halt. The world went still and Max was frozen with it, pinned into place as Allegra's words rang in his head.

When did you first realise that you were in love with me?

He couldn't be in love with Allegra, Max thought in panic. There was some mistake. He'd put his hand up to momentary lust perhaps, but *love*? No, no, no, no. She was pretending, Max reminded himself with a touch of desperation. She didn't really believe he was in love with her.

So why had her words settled into place in his head as if they belonged there?

Allegra turned in her seat so that Bob and Karen couldn't see her give him a warning dead-eye look. 'Was it when I let you paint my toenails?' she asked.

Paint…? What? Max's brows snapped together until he

realised belatedly that she was trying to prod him into responding. God knew what his expression had looked like as he'd sat there, stunned at the realisation that he had, in fact, fallen in love with Allegra.

Fool that he was.

But not so foolish he would humiliate himself by letting anyone guess, Allegra least of all.

Max recovered himself with an effort. 'I think it was more when I realised how distraught you were at the idea of me going to Shofrar,' he said, pretending to consider the matter. He looked at Bob and Karen. 'It was only then I understood just what I meant to her.'

There was a whack on his arm. 'I was not distraught!' Allegra said indignantly.

'You were weeping and wailing and begging me not to go, remember?'

'You are such a big fibber!' she protested, but she was laughing too.

'*I'm* a fibber? What was that about me painting your toenails?'

'I never cry,' she insisted to Karen, who looked from one to the other in amusement.

'Well, however you fell in love, I can just tell that you two are perfect together!'

'We think so, don't we, sweetheart?' That was Allegra again, playing it for all it was worth. She leant confidingly towards Karen. 'Of course, Max can be a bit grumpy at times, but I know he adores me.'

The little minx.

Fortunately Bob chose that moment to ask Max about the project he was working on and Max seized on the chance to drag the conversation back to safe territory.

But Karen was asking about the wedding, and Max found it harder than he'd thought to concentrate on engineering while beside him Allegra had launched into a vivid description of an imaginary wedding ceremony, her dress, what the bridesmaids would be wearing, how the tables would be decorated, and a host of other details that Max had never even considered in connection with a wedding.

He listened incredulously with one ear. Where did Allegra *get* all this stuff from? Oh, God, now she was sketching outfits on the back of an envelope she'd dug out of her jewelled bag and Karen was oohing and aahing.

'Oh, that's darling!' she exclaimed, and in spite of himself Max craned his neck to see what Allegra had drawn. There she stood in a slender dress with a low wide neckline and that was unmistakably him next to her, dressed in a morning suit and a *flowery waistcoat*.

'Over my dead body,' he muttered in Allegra's ear, and she pressed her lips together but he could see her body shaking with suppressed giggles.

'Women and weddings, huh?' said Bob as Max caught his eye. 'Take my advice, just go along with whatever they want.'

'I guess your mom will want to be involved in the wedding plans too?' Karen said to Allegra, ignoring the men.

'Er, yes.' Max could see Allegra trying to imagine poring over table decorations with Flick. 'Yes, she will, of course, but really it's just between Max and me, isn't it?'

'Quite right,' said Bob, 'and the sooner you get on with it the better, am I right, Max? But I'm not sure you're going to have time to get married before you go out to Shofrar. You'll have to come back for the wedding.'

Max looked at Bob and then at Allegra, whose face lit with excitement. 'Does that mean…?' she asked Bob, and he nodded and smiled.

'Sure. Of course Max gets the job.'

Allegra squealed with excitement and flung her

arms around Max. 'Oh, Max, you got it! You're going to Shofrar!'

Her cheek was pressed against his, and unthinkingly his arms closed around her, pulling her tight. Bob and Karen were watching indulgently and when Allegra turned her head and smiled, it seemed the most natural thing in the world to kiss her.

Her mouth was soft and lusciously curved and so close it would have been rude not to, in fact. And it would look good, Max thought hazily, unable to wrench his gaze from her lips. The Laskovskis were expecting him to kiss Allegra. That was what engaged couples did when they got good news. It would seem odd if he *didn't* kiss her.

One hand slid up her spine to the nape of her neck. For one still moment he looked straight into the deep, mossy green of Allegra's eyes and all rational thought evaporated. There was nothing but her warmth, her scent, her mouth.

Her *mouth*.

He couldn't resist any longer. He'd forgotten why he needed to, forgotten everything but the need to seal the gap between them. He drew her head towards him—or perhaps she leant closer; Max never knew—and angled his lips against hers, and the taste and the touch of her blew his senses apart so that he could almost have sworn that the restaurant swung wildly around them.

She was warm and responsive, pliant against him, and their mouths fitted together as if they were meant for each other. The astonishing rightness of it rose in his chest and surged through him like a tide, blocking out doubts, blocking out reason, blocking out everything that wasn't Allegra: the scent of her, the feel of her, the sweetness of her.

Afterwards, Max calculated that the kiss couldn't have lasted more than a few seconds, but at the time it seemed to stretch to infinity and beyond. He never knew where he found the strength to pull away, but somehow he had drawn back and was staring into her eyes once more. The lovely green was dark and dazed, and her expression was as stunned as his must have been.

'Yep,' said Bob to Karen, 'the sooner those two get married the better, I'd say.'

Desperately, Max tried to pull himself together. His blood was pounding, which was crazy. It had just been a kiss, hardly more than a peck on the lips. There was no reason for his heart to be throbbing still like that, for his lungs to have forgotten how to function.

He had to get a grip, focus on the job. He had what he wanted. He was going to Shofrar to be a project manager, just like he had planned. He ought to be elated, not thinking about the way Allegra's words were ringing in his ears: *You're going to Shofrar*, she had exclaimed in delight.

You're going, not *we're going*.

They were all picking up their glasses and Bob was toasting Max's promotion. Max stretched his mouth into a smile.

You, not *we*.

That was how it should be, Max told himself. In a few weeks, he would get on a plane and fly out to the desert and Allegra wouldn't be there. He would get on with his life and she would get on with hers. Their lives were on separate tracks, heading in different directions.

If Libby ever got married, they might meet at her wedding or the occasional christening but that was far in the future. They might have forgotten this evening by then, forgotten that kiss, or perhaps they would share a wry smile at the memory. It wouldn't matter then.

Max couldn't imagine it.

He stole a glance at Allegra. She looked as if she had forgotten it already, he thought with resentment. *She* wasn't flailing off balance. There was a faint flush along her cheekbones, but otherwise she seemed perfectly composed as she chatted to Karen.

'What are you going to do with yourself in Shofrar, Allegra?' Karen asked. 'If Max is anything like Bob, he'll be at work all day. You really need a career that can travel with you.'

Allegra opened her mouth but Max got in first. 'Allegra's an illustrator,' he said. 'She's going to write and illustrate children's books.'

'Really?' Karen was fascinated but Allegra was already shaking her head.

'Oh, well, I'm not sure I'm good enough,' she began.

'She's brilliant,' Max told Karen, ignoring Allegra's kick under the table. 'She just doesn't know it.'

It was true, he thought. She would be so much happier illustrating rather than running around meeting the crazy deadlines at *Glitz*, but she wouldn't change because for some reason Flick had a bee in her bonnet about Allegra's drawing. She was always putting it down, so of course Allegra thought it wasn't good enough, but Max was convinced her illustrations had something special about them.

Karen made Allegra tell her all about the book she was going to write and, in spite of the vengeful looks Allegra was sending his way, Max noticed that she had plenty of ideas. She might say that she was dedicated to journalism but she had obviously thought about the stories starring the infamous Derek the Dog. Max wished she would write the book and forget about Flick's opinion for once. Perhaps she never would in real life, but at least she could pretend to have the perfect career for this evening.

Because this evening was all they had. After tonight, the pretence was over. He had better not forget that.

Beside Max, Allegra was wishing Karen wouldn't ask quite so many interested questions about a book she had no intention of writing. They were just silly little stories she had made up, not even a real book, but Karen certainly seemed thrilled by the idea and claimed her grandchildren would love Derek the Dog. If she wasn't careful she would find herself writing the pesky thing, Allegra thought with an inner sigh. She could just imagine what Flick would think of *that*!

Perhaps she could use a pseudonym?

Aware of a flicker of excitement at the thought, Allegra pushed it firmly out of sight. She had enough going on in her head right now, what with thinking about a nonexistent book and trying *not* to think about the way Max had kissed her.

And especially not about the way she had kissed him back.

There was a disquieting prickle still at the nape of her neck where his hand had rested. Her lips felt tender, as if his had seared hers, and she kept running the tip of her tongue over them, as surreptitiously as she could, checking that they hadn't swollen.

The jolt of sensation when their mouths met had shaken her. Kissing Max wasn't supposed to feel like that. It was supposed to be a meaningless peck of the lips, the kind of kiss she gave out every day to her colleagues at *Glitz*.

It was hard to tell what Max thought about it. For one breathless moment afterwards they had stared at each other, but then his eyes had shuttered and now he was immersed in a technical discussion with Bob. He was talking about *concrete*. It wasn't fair. He shouldn't be able to kiss her and then calmly carry on discussing road building!

Karen and Bob were entertaining company and the meal was delicious, but Allegra couldn't enjoy it. She was too aware of Max, who was his usual taciturn self, and who, having kissed her and dropped her in it with Karen, had proceeded to ignore her for the rest of the evening.

It wasn't good enough, Allegra thought crossly, tapping her Jimmy Choos under the table. She had done everything he'd asked of her. She'd been charming, but Max hadn't even *tried*. If it wasn't for her, he wouldn't even *have* his rotten job, Allegra decided, but now he'd got what he wanted he had obviously decided he didn't need to bother with her any more.

Her smile was brittle by the time they said goodbye to Bob and Karen outside the restaurant. The Laskovskis were walking back to their hotel and, after one glance at Allegra's shoes, Max didn't even bother to suggest the Tube. Instead he put his fingers in his mouth and whistled at a passing taxi. If it had been Allegra, the taxi would have sailed on past in the other direction and she didn't know whether to be relieved or put-out that it responded instantly to Max's whistle, turning across the traffic and drawing up exactly in front of them.

Her feet were definitely relieved.

Haughtily, she got in and made a big performance of putting on her seat belt. Max told the taxi driver the address and settled beside her, apparently unperturbed by the taut silence. Allegra folded her lips together. *She* wasn't going to break it. She had made enough small talk for one night, thank you very much! She turned her head away and looked pointedly out of the window, but she was so aware of him sitting just a matter of inches away across the seat that she might as well have turned and stared right at him.

It wasn't even as if he was doing anything. He was just sitting still, his face in shadow, his eyes fixed on the ticking taxi meter. He could at least jiggle his leg or do something annoying so that she had an excuse to snap at him.

As it was, she was just getting crosser and crosser, and more and more frustrated.

Why, why, why had he had to kiss her like that? It had been all right up to then. The pretence had been fun and she had been able to dismiss her bizarre awareness of him as a temporary aberration, a passing symptom of sexual frustration. Nothing that meant anything, anyway. She'd been able to think of him as just Max.

He'd spoiled everything by kissing her. It had been so perfect, as if her whole life had just been about getting her to that place, that moment, where everything else had fallen away and there had just been her and Max and a longing for it never to end gusting through her.

How could she think of him as just Max now?

She wished he'd never kissed her.

She wished he'd kiss her again.

The realisation of just how much she wanted it made Allegra suck in her breath. This was mad. She was furious with Max. She couldn't want to kiss him at the same time. She couldn't want him to reach across and pull her towards him, couldn't want his hands on her, his mouth on her, not when he'd ignored her all night and clearly had no interest in kissing *her* again.

But she did.

The silence lengthened, stretched agonizingly. Just when Allegra opened her mouth to break it, unable to bear it any longer, Max let out a sigh.

'I'm sorry,' he said simply.

At least it gave her the excuse to turn and look at him. 'Sorry?' she echoed, unable to stop the pent-up frustration from tumbling out. 'I should think so! Do you have any idea how hard I worked all evening to suck up to the Laskovskis? I got you your bloody job all by myself!'

'I know,' Max began, but Allegra wasn't stopping now that she had started.

'You hardly said a word all evening—oh, except to embarrass me by telling Karen I was going to write a book! What did you do that for?'

'I think you should write one. I think it would be brilliant.'

Allegra wasn't going to be mollified. 'It would not be! It would be stupid! I had to sit there and pretend that I was all excited about it and now Karen's expecting me to send her a copy when it's published! It's not funny,' she added furiously, spotting the ghost of a smile hovering around Max's mouth. 'I felt an absolute fool. As if it wasn't bad enough pretending to be in love with you!'

'You did it really well,' said Max. 'You were brilliant at that too, and you're right, you got me the job. Thank you,' he said quietly. 'Really, Allegra: thank you.'

Perversely, his gratitude just made her feel worse. She hunched a shoulder. 'I only did it so that you'd do the article.' She sounded petulant, but that was how she felt.

'I know.'

'But you could have helped,' she grumbled. 'You were useless! I can't believe the Laskovskis were taken in. A real fiancé would have looked at me, maybe smiled occasionally, taken every opportunity to get close to me, but not you! It was like you couldn't bear to touch me.'

'That's not true,' said Max tautly. 'I kissed you.'

As if she could have forgotten!

'Only when I threw myself into your arms! *Pretending* to be a loving fiancée, thrilled for her future husband's promotion,' Allegra added quickly, just in case he had misinterpreted her instinctive reaction. She had been so pleased for him too, she remembered bitterly. 'Although I don't know why I bothered. You gave the impression you'd rather have been picking up slugs!'

'What?' Max sounded so staggered that Allegra wondered if she might have exaggerated a little, but she had gone too far to back down now. Besides, she had been bottling it up all evening and it was good to get it off her chest.

'I might as well have been a pillar of your precious concrete for all the notice you took of me all evening!'

Max uttered a strangled laugh and dragged a hand through his hair. 'It wasn't like that,' he began.

'Then why did you ignore me?'

'Because I didn't trust myself, all right?' he shouted, goaded at last. 'Because if I hadn't ignored you, I wouldn't have been able to keep my hands off you! I'd have kissed you again and again and I wouldn't have been able to stop. I'd have dragged you down under the table and ripped that bloody dress off you so I could kiss you all over your body and to hell with my boss sitting there with his wife and the rest of the restaurant...'

He broke off. His chest was heaving and he looked wild-eyed as he glared at Allegra. 'So now you know. There, are you satisfied now?'

'But...but...' It was Allegra's turn to gape.

'Of course I wanted to touch you!' Max said furiously. 'I've wanted it ever since you opened the bathroom door. I haven't been able to think about anything else all evening. I had to sit there, trying to talk to my boss, when all I could think about was how easy it would be to slide my hand under your dress, about how it would feel to unzip it, all the time knowing it would never happen! And you wanted me to do chit-chat as well?'

He was glowering at her as if he hated her, but a treacherous warmth was stealing along Allegra's veins, dissolving her own anger into something far more dangerous, while the spikiness in the atmosphere evaporated into quite a different kind of tension.

He wanted her.

Desire twisted sharp and sure in her belly. His hair was standing on end where he had raked his hand through it and he looked cross, rumpled, *gorgeous*. When had he become so…so…so *hot*? Why hadn't she noticed?

Allegra's heart thudded in her throat and her mouth dried with a mixture of anticipation and apprehension. She had been sent once to try bungee jumping for an article and she had felt just like this when she'd stood on the edge of the bridge: terrified, thrilled, longing to be brave enough to jump but afraid that she would never have the courage.

She had done it, though. She could do this too, if she really wanted to. Allegra moistened her lips.

Max wanted her.

She wanted him.

Allegra's mind was still busy calculating the risk when her mouth opened and she heard herself say, 'How do you know?'

Thrown, Max stared at her. 'How do I know what?'

'That it would never happen.' Allegra watched, appalled, as her body took over, shifting towards him, reaching out for his hand, setting it on her knee, all without a single instruction from her brain.

What was she *doing*? she thought in panic, but her hands seemed to have acquired a will of their own. *Stop it*, she told herself frantically, but the message wasn't getting through, and now her legs were getting in on the act, quaking with pleasure at the warm weight of his hand.

Max swallowed. 'I'm not sure this is a good idea, Legs,' he said in a constricted voice, but he didn't seem to have any better control over his hands than she did. His fingers were curling over her knee, pressing through her sheer tights into the soft skin of her inner thigh, and she couldn't prevent the shudder of response clenching at the base of her spine.

'I'm not sure either,' she admitted with difficulty. She willed her knees to press together and squeeze out his hand but they wouldn't cooperate.

'It could be that we're just getting carried away by the pretence,' Max said but he didn't lift his hand. Instead his knuckles nudged aside the hem of her dress so that he could stroke higher inside her thigh.

Allegra felt lust crawling deeper, digging in. It would take over completely if she didn't regain control, but his skimming fingers were searing such delicious patterns on her skin she couldn't think clearly.

'Bound to be that,' she agreed breathlessly. 'And the whole article thing. It's getting a bit out of hand. We're spending too much time together.'

'Yep,' said Max, as his fingers played on the inside of her thigh, higher, higher, higher, until Allegra squirmed in her seat. 'We should stop right now.'

'We should,' she managed.

'Unless...'

'Yes?' Her breathing was too choppy to get anything else out.

'Unless we get it out of our system,' Max suggested. Had his voice always been that deep, that darkly delicious? 'Just one night, and then we can forget all about it. What do you think?'

Think? How could she be expected to think when his fingers were stroking so exquisitely that she couldn't breathe properly and she was giddy with the dark plea-sure of it? Oh, God, if his hand went any higher, she would come apart.

If it didn't, she would explode. Either way, they would end up with a horrible mess all over the taxi seat.

Struggling to stop herself pressing down into his hand, she scrabbled for some words to put together. 'I think… that's…a good idea…' she gasped and Max smiled, a wicked smile she hadn't known he possessed.

When he withdrew his hand, Allegra almost moaned in protest before she realised that the taxi had stopped in front of the house. Max paid the driver while she made it waveringly to the front door on legs that felt boneless.

She was still fumbling with the keys as Max came up behind her. Wordlessly, he took them from her and opened the door.

'After you,' he said, but there was a telltale hitch in his voice that made Allegra feel obscurely better. So it wasn't just her having trouble breathing.

She didn't want to put on the hall light, so she waited, trembling with anticipation, in the dark until Max had closed the door behind them. A muted orange glow from the street lights outside filtered through the glass pane above the door. It was enough to see him turn, see the gleam of his smile as he moved towards her, and then his hands were on her and at last—at last!—his mouth came down on hers, angling desperate and demanding.

This time there was none of the piercing sweetness she had felt in the restaurant. Instead his kiss was hot and fierce, and Allegra felt need explode inside her, vaporising the last lingering remnants of rational thought. Her mind went dark and she kissed him back, wild with hunger, wanting his hands on her harder, hotter, *harder*.

No, there was no sweetness now. It felt like more of a struggle as to who needed most, who could give most, who could take most. Allegra scrabbled for his tie, at the buttons on his shirt, while his hands pushed up her dress urgently and his mouth blazed a trail to her breast. The hunger rocketed through her, so powerful it thrilled and terrified her in equal measure, and when they broke apart the narrow hallway echoed with the rasp of their ragged breaths.

Chest heaving, Max pressed their palms together and lifted their arms slowly above her head so that he could pin her against the wall.

'We're going to regret this,' he said, even as he bent his head to kiss her throat, making every cell in her body jolt, turning her insides molten.

'I know.'

'It's crazy.' His lips drifted downward in a searing trail over her skin that left her breathing in tatters.

'You're right,' she managed, sucking in a gasp as he explored the sensitive curve of her neck and shoulder and arching into the wicked pleasure of his mouth.

When he released her wrists to jerk her closer, she whimpered with relief. Now she could tug his shirt free so that she could slide her palms over his firm, smooth back, letting herself notice how his muscles flexed beneath her touch. He was gloriously solid, wonderfully warm. She wanted to burrow into him, lose herself in him.

'It'll just spoil things,' she said unevenly, holding onto the track of the conversation with difficulty.

'It will. It'll never be the same again,' said Max, his voice low and ragged. 'I'm never going to be able to forget how you taste,' he warned her. 'I'll never forget how you feel, how soft you are.'

'So…we should stop,' she tried, even as she pressed him closer, revelling in the feel of how hard he was, how strong, how male. Her blood was thumping and thudding and throbbing with urgency and she wanted him so much that she couldn't think about anything else.

'We probably should,' said Max, his hands sliding

under her dress, his mouth hot on her skin. 'But there's a problem.'

Allegra shuddered under his touch. 'A…a problem?'

'Yes.' He lifted his head and brought his hands up to frame her face. 'The problem is, I don't want to stop, do you?'

She ought to say yes. She ought to put a stop to this right now. Max was right. They would regret this in the morning. But how could she say stop when her body was arching towards his and her skin yearned for his touch and her blood was running wild and wanting him blotted out everything else?

Her arms wrapped round his neck and she pulled him closer for a deep, wet kiss. 'No,' she murmured against his lips, 'I don't want to stop.'

CHAPTER EIGHT

ALLEGRA SURFACED SLOWLY to an awareness of an unfamiliar weight lying across her waist. She blinked at a bedside table. Not hers. The arm thrown over her wasn't hers either. A warm male body was pressed against her back, a face buried in her hair. Steady breath stirred the air against her shoulder and she quivered as memory came whooshing back.

Max. Omigod, she had slept with Max!

Now what was she going to do?

Allegra lay very still. Max was sound asleep and she didn't want to wake him until she had worked out how she was going to react.

Could she pretend that she'd had too much to drink? But she had known exactly what she was doing, and Max knew it.

Okay, so she'd be casual. *Thank goodness we've got that out of our system, now we can move on*: that kind of thing.

Only being casual wasn't going to be easy when she'd just had the best sex of her life. Her body was still buzzing pleasantly in the aftermath, and she flushed at the memory of the careening excitement, the heart-shaking pleasure that had left her languid and replete at last.

It would be so much easier if the sex had been disappointing, or even average. If Max had been a pedestrian lover, as conventional and dull as his suits. Instead…Allegra's blood tingled, remembering the shattering sureness of his hands, of his mouth…oh, God, *his mouth*… In spite of herself, her lips curved. Who would have thought that the crisp and efficient engineer was capable of *that*?

How much more passion had Emma wanted?

Allegra wished she hadn't thought about Emma. She'd been on the verge of turning over and waking Max, but now she'd remembered reality. Last night hadn't changed anything. Max would be going to Shofrar soon, and if he took anyone with him it wouldn't be his sister's frivolous, fashionable friend.

And Libby! That was another complication. How would she feel if she knew Allegra had slept with her brother? But Allegra couldn't keep a secret from her best friend. Allegra gnawed her bottom lip. She wished she could rewind the hours and go back to the night, to the darkness where nothing had mattered but touch and feel and taste, the glorious slide of flesh against flesh, the spiralling excitement, the splintering joy.

What time was it anyway? Very cautiously, Allegra reached towards the phone on the bedside table. Sensing her movement in his sleep, Max mumbled a protest and tightened his arm about her, pulling her back against his hard body. It felt so good that Allegra's heart contracted, but she made herself wriggle free and grope once more for the phone.

Her fingers closed round it and she peered at the screen: 08:45. Holy smoke!

'Max!' She sat bolt upright in bed. 'Max, wake up! It's nearly nine o'clock!'

'Wha…?' Max struggled up, scowling at the abrupt awakening. His eyes were screwed up, his hair ruffled. Allegra wanted to take his face between her hands and kiss the grouchiness away. She wanted to push him down into the pillows and lose herself in his touch.

Instead she leapt out of bed, out of temptation. 'I'm going to be late!' she said, scrabbling frantically for her clothes. She found a bra, a pair of tights... What the hell had happened to her dress?

'Wait...' The sleep was clearing from Max's face and his expression changed as he watched Allegra pounce on the dress that lay in a puddle on the floor, where it had fallen last night. He had a vivid memory of unzipping it slowly, of listening to the enticing rustle as it slithered down over Allegra's hips, of catching his breath at the sight of her in a black push-up bra and lacy thong.

'Allegra, wait,' he said again as memory after memory of the night before flashed through his mind like an erotic slide show.

She turned, tousle-haired, wide-eyed, clutching her pile of clothes to her chest, forgetting that it was a little late for modesty. 'Didn't you hear what I said? It's nearly nine!'

'Nearly *nine*?' This time it got through. He scrambled out of bed, stark naked. 'Shit! I was supposed to be at work half an hour ago!'

'You can have the shower first,' she said. 'You're quicker than me.'

Max hesitated, dragged a hand through his hair. He was *never* late for work, but he couldn't leave it like that. He might not have thought ahead last night, but he knew the morning wasn't supposed to be like this, and he found himself saying the words he never thought he would hear coming out of his mouth: 'We need to talk.'

'I know,' said Allegra, not quite meeting his eyes, 'but later.'

Perhaps later was better, Max told himself as he showered and shaved as quickly as he could, which was pretty damn quickly. By the evening he might have had a chance to get a grip of himself. It would have been too hard to talk with Allegra's scent still clogging his brain, with his heart still thundering with the memory of her sweetness, her warmth, her wicked, irresistible smile. She had turned him upside down, inside out.

She had turned him wild.

Max shrugged on his shirt, knotted his tie, dressed himself in his civilised suit, but underneath he still felt stripped bare. He'd been unprepared for the wildness of his need for her, for the way the feel of her set something free inside him.

So free that he'd lost his mind, lost himself. Max set his jaw, remembering the foolishness he'd spouted, the incoherent words that had tumbled out of him as they'd moved together, up and up through swirling darkness towards the shattering light. He hadn't known what he was saying, but now the words were out, how the hell was he going to put them back?

He was at the round table, filling out a visa form for Shofrar, when Allegra got home that night. The moment he heard the key in the door, every cell in his body seemed to leap in anticipation, but he had his expression well under control by the time she appeared in the doorway.

There was a pause, then Allegra said, 'Hi.'

'You're back late.' Max hated the accusing note in his own voice. Anyone would think that he was keeping track of her, that he'd been sitting here, just waiting for her to come home.

'I've been to the launch of a new jewellery collection.' Allegra hesitated, then came into the room. She was wearing skinny leopard-print jeans, a tight T-shirt and a leather jacket, with chunky earrings and shiny boots. Her hair was pulled back in one of those messy twists that Max disliked. She looked funky, hip, a million miles from the elegant woman who'd taken his arm last night.

From the woman who'd short-circuited every single one of his fuses last night.

She unzipped her jacket and dropped her bag on the sofa. 'What are you doing?' she asked, perching on the arm so that she could take off her boots.

'A visa application for Shofrar,' said Max.

Allegra glanced up from her right boot. 'Already?'

'I saw Bob Laskovski again today. One of the project managers out there has been in a car accident. He's okay, I think, but they're bringing him back to hospital here. Bob wanted to know if I could go out earlier.'

She stilled. 'How much earlier?'

'The end of next week.'

'Oh.'

'Bob was asking about wedding dates,' said Max, relieved to hear that he sounded so normal. 'He was anxious to reassure me that I could come back in a month or so to sort stuff out, and that you could join me whenever you're ready.'

'I see,' said Allegra. She bent her head and went back to fiddling with her boot. 'Well…that's good. You must be pleased.'

'Yes,' said Max. He should be delighted. This was exactly what he had wanted, after all. So why didn't he *feel* pleased?

He wished Allegra would look up. He wished she didn't look so trendy. He wished they hadn't started on this awful stilted conversation when they should be talking about the night before. 'What about your article? Can we fit in the last tests by next week?'

She pursed her lips, considering, apparently unbothered

by the fact that he would be leaving so soon. 'I've arranged with Darcy that you'll go with her to the opening of the new Digby Fox exhibition on Tuesday evening,' she said.

'Who's Digby Fox?' he said, disgruntled.

'Only the hottest ticket in the art world at the moment. He's a really controversial artist but anyone who's anyone will be there to look at his new installations.'

'And Darcy wants to go to this?' Max couldn't hide his scepticism.

'She wants to change her image and be taken more seriously. And Digby Fox is really interesting,' she told him. 'But that would be your last challenge. The costume ball isn't for another month, you'll be gutted to hear, so you'll miss that.'

'What, no waltzing after all?'

'No.' Allegra's smile was a little painful.

'I'm sorry,' said Max.

'No you're not,' she said, sounding much more herself. 'You told me you'd rather stick pins in your eyes than waltz.'

'I'm sorry to let you down,' he clarified. 'I promised I'd do it.'

'It can't be helped. If you can make it to the Digby Fox preview I'll have enough material,' she said. 'It's a shame about the ball, but maybe I'll ask William if he'd go with Darcy. I'm sure he knows how to waltz.'

William? Max bristled at her careless assumption that he could be so easily replaced. The last thing he'd wanted to do was make a fool of himself at some stupid ball, but still…

Allegra was being exasperatingly reasonable. Why couldn't she go all dramatic and start weeping and wailing about the tragedy of her unfinished article? Max would feel so much better if she did. All this politeness was getting to him. They needed to stop this and talk about the night before.

'Look, Legs,' he began but, before he could finish, his phone started to ring. Max cursed.

'Aren't you going to get that?'

'It can go to voicemail.'

'It might be important.'

Muttering under his breath, he snatched up the phone and looked at the screen in disbelief.

'Who is it?' asked Allegra.

'It's Emma,' he said slowly.

Allegra got up, dropping her left boot on the floor. 'You should talk to her,' she said. 'I'm going to get changed anyway.'

She left her boots lying as they were, and Max watched, churning with frustration, as she walked out barefoot. The boots looked as abandoned and forlorn as he felt, and Max bent to put them neatly side by side as he pressed the answer button on his phone.

'Hello?' he said.

In her room, Allegra leant back against the door and drew a deep breath. That had gone better than she'd feared. She'd been calm, cool. She hadn't cried. She hadn't thrown herself into his arms and begged him not to go, although it had been a close run thing when he'd told her that he was going to Shofrar next week.

Next week.

It was all for the best, Allegra told herself. Let's face it, last night had been a one-off. It had been incredible, amazingly so, but they were still the same people as they'd been before, who had different lives and wanted different things. Of course it was tempting to imagine that they could recreate the previous night, but really, what would

be the point? It would just make it harder to say goodbye
in a week's time.

Emma had rung at just the right time. She was what
Max really needed. Allegra hoped that she was telling
Max that she had made a terrible mistake and wanted to
go back to him. She really did.

A nasty headache was jabbing right behind her eyes
and her throat felt tight. Allegra pulled the clip from her
hair and changed her tight jeans for a pair of pyjama bottoms patterned with faded puppies, sighing at the comfort.
Wrapping a soft grey cardigan around her, she padded back
down to the kitchen and poured herself a bowl of cereal.
She was tempted to eat it there but it felt like avoiding
Max, and that would make it seem as if last night was a
big deal, which it wasn't at all. Besides, she hadn't heard
his voice when she passed the sitting room door, so pre-
sumably he'd finished talking to Emma.

Sure enough, when she carried her bowl back to the living room Max was sitting at the table once more, but he
wasn't filling in his form. He was staring ahead, turning
his pen abstractedly between his fingers. He looked tired,
and a dangerous rush of emotion gusted through Allegra.

What would it be like if she could go over and massage
his shoulders? Would he jerk away in horror, or would he
let his head drop back against her breasts? Would he let
her slide her arms down to his chest so that she could press
her lips to his jaw and kiss his throat the way she had done
the night before?

Allegra's chest was so tight that for a moment she
couldn't move. She could just stand in the doorway in her
old pyjama bottoms and the sleeves of her cardigan falling
over her hands, and when Max glanced up and their eyes

met the jolt in the air was so unexpected that she jerked, slopping the milk in the bowl of cereal she held.

'Allegra…' After that one frozen moment, Max pushed back his chair abruptly and got to his feet, only to stop as if he had forgotten what he was going to say.

'How was Emma?' Allegra rushed to fill the silence. She slouched over to the sofa and stretched out on it to eat her cereal, deliberately casual.

Max hesitated. 'She wants to meet.'

'Hey, that's great news!'

'Is it?'

'Of course it is.' Allegra kept beaming, which was quite hard when you were trying to eat cereal at the same time. 'Come on, Max, you want her back. You know you do.'

'If I wanted her that much, I wouldn't have slept with you last night,' he said.

'That didn't mean anything. We both agreed that.' Deliberately she finished her cereal, scraping around the bowl, not looking at Max. Just another slobby evening, nothing on her mind.

'We knew what were doing,' she persevered when Max said nothing. 'It was meant to be a bit of fun, wasn't it?— and it *was*, but it's not as if either of us want a relationship. We know each other too well for that. We'd drive each other mad!'

Allegra had been practising this speech all day, but Max didn't seem impressed. He came over to the sofa, took the bowl from her unresisting hand and set it on the table. Then he nudged her legs so that she lifted them for him to sit down.

Just the way she had nudged his that night she had looked at him and decided that he was perfect for her article. Allegra almost winced at the jab of memory as she settled her legs across his lap. She had thought she had known Max then, but she hadn't had a clue. She'd known nothing about the clean male scent of his skin or the enticing scrape of his jaw. Nothing about the lean, lovely strength of his body or the dark, delicious pleasure of his hands. Nothing about how it felt when his mouth curved against her flesh.

Max studied the puppies on her pyjama bottoms a moment then lifted his eyes to hers. 'What if I *did* want a relationship, Legs?' he said, and the last of Allegra's breath leaked out of her lungs.

'You're…not serious?' she managed.

'Why not?'

'Because it's crazy. You said it yourself last night. Madness, you said. We'll regret it in the morning, you said.'

'I know I did,' he said evenly. 'But the thing is, I didn't regret it. I still don't.'

'Max…'

'Do you regret it?' he asked her and Allegra couldn't look away, couldn't lie.

'No. No, I don't.'

He stroked one of her bare feet thoughtfully, making her suck in a sharp breath. 'Then why don't we try it again? We might not regret that either.'

His hand was warm and firm and she could have sworn she felt his touch in every molecule. Unable to prevent a quiver of response, she made herself pull the foot away and draw up her legs.

'It was just sex,' she said, keeping her voice steady with an effort. 'It was great, don't get me wrong, but I don't think we should read more into it than that.'

'Okay,' said Max. 'So why don't we have great sex until I leave?'

'Because…' Couldn't he *see*? 'Because it's too hard to stop great sex becoming something else, and then where would we be?'

'In a relationship?'

'And what would be the point of that? You're going to Shofrar next week?'

'No, you're right,' Max said. 'What was I thinking?'

'I know what you were thinking *with*,' said Allegra in an effort to lighten the conversation, and a smile tugged at the corner of his mouth.

'Maybe,' he said.

'It *was* lovely,' she said, unable to keep the wistful note from creeping into her voice, 'but I can't see me in the desert, can you?'

'No,' he said slowly. 'No, I can't.'

'You need someone like Emma,' Allegra ploughed on, struggling to remember the script she had prepared. 'Someone who can really be part of your life.' Someone not like me, she added bleakly to herself. 'I'm sure that when you meet her again you'll remember just how important she was to you before. It's only a couple of months since you wanted to marry her,' she reminded him. 'You need to think about what really matters to you and let's go back to being friends.'

'And last night?'

No wonder she hadn't spent any time being sensible before. Being sensible hurt. But it didn't hurt as much as falling in love with him would hurt, or the inevitable moment when Max would realise that sex wasn't enough, that *she* wasn't enough.

Just like she hadn't been enough to keep her unknown father around.

Like she was never quite enough to please her mother.

Allegra drew a breath and summoned a smile. 'Last night wasn't real,' she said. 'It was lovely, but I think it would be easier if we pretended that it never happened.'

Pretend it never happened. Easy for *her* to say! Max yanked his tie savagely into place. Bloody Dickie had picked out another humdinger for him to wear to the preview of Digby Fox's exhibition: a fluorescent green shirt with a red tie, and a tweed jacket in hunter green.

'It's bold, it's assertive, it's *you*,' Dickie had assured him when Max had refused absolutely to consider any of it. 'Just try it,' he had coaxed and in the end, Max had given in for a quiet life. It was the last time he'd have to make a fool of himself, after all.

Dickie had been on the verge of tears when he'd heard that Max wouldn't be going to the costume ball after all.

'I had *such* a marvellous outfit in mind for you too,' he'd mourned.

Another reason to be grateful that he was going to Shofrar early, Max decided as he dressed grimly.

Allegra had cancelled their dancing lessons, which meant that he never needed to waltz again. And what a relief *that* was! He wasn't missing those lessons at all. If he had found himself remembering the times he and Allegra had practised twirling around the room, it was only because he felt bad at letting her down. He knew how much she had been looking forward to the ball.

Now she would be going with William.

Not that he cared that Allegra had been able to replace him so easily, Max reassured himself hastily. He was well out of it.

He regarded his reflection glumly. He looked a total prat. The neon-green shirt made him look as if he should be directing traffic. At least Dickie had had to accept his refusal to grow a designer stubble. Max rubbed a hand over his freshly shaven jaw. The truth was, he'd nearly given way on that too when he'd realised how disappointed Dickie was that Max wouldn't be able to take him to a rugby match the way he'd promised.

He seemed to be letting everyone down at the moment.

With a sigh, he picked up the jacket Dickie had assured him was the last word in style and headed for the door. He was to meet Allegra and Darcy at the gallery. Max couldn't say that he was looking forward to the evening ahead, but he'd done his homework. Allegra had pressed a book on modern art into his hands so that he would impress Darcy with his knowledge but, having ploughed through it, he was none the wiser. He would just have to wing it, he decided. He could look thoughtful and mumble something about challenging perceptions and that would have to do.

And, after tonight, his obligations would be over. He could concentrate on handing over his projects at work and pack up the few belongings he'd brought with him when he'd moved out of Emma's. Everything was already stored in the attic in his parents' house. Max had been home to say goodbye to his parents that weekend so that he didn't get in Allegra's way, but it hadn't been as restful as he'd hoped. His mother had an uncanny ability to home in on the things Max least wanted to talk about and she kept asking how Allegra was and how they were getting on sharing the house. Max tried an austere 'fine' in reply, but oh, no, that wasn't enough.

'What aren't you telling me?' she'd demanded.

She didn't seem to understand that there were some things you couldn't tell your mother.

He couldn't tell her about the way his breath clogged every time he looked at Allegra. He couldn't tell her about the memories that circled obsessively in his head, memories of the hot, sweet darkness, of the pleasure that had leapt like wildfire, consuming everything in its path. He couldn't tell her how the feel of Allegra had blotted everything else from his mind.

'Allegra is fine,' he'd insisted to his mother.

Allegra certainly seemed fine. She was doing a lot better than he was, anyway.

She'd been bright and brittle ever since she'd sat on the sofa looking soft and oh-so-touchable in those silly pyjamas. Max's hands had itched to slide beneath the faded material, to peel that baggy cardigan from her shoulders and lay her down beneath him once more, but the moment he'd succumbed to temptation and stroked her foot, she had pulled away.

Last night wasn't real, she'd said. *Let's pretend it never happened.*

Max hadn't tried to change her mind. Allegra had made it clear that she didn't want him to touch her again, and he wasn't about to start forcing himself on a woman. She might have dressed it all up as wanting him to be happy, but Max wasn't a fool. What she meant was that she wouldn't be happy with him.

And, anyway, she was right. It was all for the best. He *couldn't* imagine Allegra in Shofrar. She wanted to stay in London, in the gossipy, glamorous world that was *Glitz*. What could he offer compared to that? A prefabricated house on a compound in the desert. Big deal.

So Max was doing his best to behave normally. He wasn't going to follow her around making puppy dog eyes. A man had his pride, after all. He met Emma for lunch and thought about what Allegra had said about Emma being what he needed. It seemed hard to remember now, but Max was prepared to try and Emma herself was dropping hints about the possibility of getting back together. Max told

Allegra that he and Emma were 'talking' and she seemed delighted, he remembered sourly.

At least he'd made someone happy.

His mood was not improved when he made it to the gallery and found Allegra already there with Darcy and a smarmy-looking man who Allegra introduced as William.

Max disliked him on sight. William had the lean, well-bred air of a greyhound. He had floppy hair and tortoise-shell glasses, which Max privately decided were fake and designed purely to make him look intelligent. And God, the man could talk! Darcy hung on his every word as William pontificated. He had an opinion on everything, as far as Max could make out. Max would have liked him a lot better if he'd taken one look at the pile of pooh on display and admitted that he didn't have a clue what it was all about.

Every surface in the gallery was painted white which was disorientating. Max was glad he didn't suffer from seasickness or he'd have been desperate for a horizon. Not that anyone else seemed to notice how weird the décor was. The gallery was jam-packed with trendy types clutching glasses of champagne. They were all talking at the tops of their voices and vying for the accolade of most preten-tious comment of the evening. Clearly it was going to be a stiff competition.

Max himself was profoundly unimpressed by the so-called 'art' on display. As far as he could see, the 'artist' had run around gathering together as much junk as he could find, thrown it into piles and called it an installa-tion. There was more art in a beautifully designed bridge than this claptrap, in Max's humble opinion.

William disagreed. He appointed himself guide and in-sisted on explaining every exhibit. Phrases like 'implicit sexual innuendo', 'aesthetic encounter' and 'anthropomor-phic narratives' fell from his lips, while Darcy hung on every word. Allegra seemed distracted, though, and Max couldn't help wondering if she was jealous of the way William was so obviously basking in Darcy's attention.

That evening she was wearing a floaty skirt, clumpy boots and short tweedy jacket. Max wanted to think that she looked a mess, but somehow she looked as if she belonged there in a way he never would, neon shirt or no neon shirt. She had plenty of her old pizazz about her, but there was a tight look around her eyes and her smile wasn't as bright as usual.

'You okay?' he asked her as William steered Darcy on to the next exhibit.

'Yes. Why?'

'I don't know. You look a bit…tired.'

Great. Everyone knew that looking 'tired' meant you looked a wreck. The chatter bouncing off the white walls was making Allegra's head ache. She felt like a wreck too.

Usually she loved these gossipy, trendy affairs, but there were too many people crammed into the gallery and it felt claustrophobic in spite of the attempts to make the design feel airy and spacious. She had to squeeze her way through the throng. Digby Fox could pull in some A-list names. So far she had muttered 'sorry…excuse me…' to minor royalty, a prize-winning author and a celebrity chef. Ordinarily, Allegra would have been thrilled, but the only person she had eyes for was Max, who was looking resolutely out of place.

How on earth had Dickie persuaded him into that shirt? It was so loud it wasn't doing anything for her headache.

Allegra had had a tiring day listening to Dickie moaning about how much he was going to miss Max. Max had shown him how to order a pint in the pub; Max had introduced him to takeaway curry; Max had promised to take him to a rugby match. He seemed to hold her personally responsible for Max's promotion.

Max made love to me! Allegra had wanted to shout. *I'm going to miss him much, much more than you.*

She didn't, of course. Dickie was still Dickie and her career was all she had to hold onto at the moment.

'You should have said *non*,' Dickie had grumbled in the accent Max swore was put on. 'Non, ze article isn't finished, you cannot go yet.'

If only it had been that easy.

She had tried to convince him that she had enough for an article, but Dickie had been counting on dressing Max for the costume ball. ''e would 'ave looked *magnifique*,' he said forlornly.

Allegra secretly thought that was unlikely. Max would never be handsome. He would never be magnificent. He was quietly austere and understated and ordinary and she wanted him more than anything she had ever wanted in her life.

And, oh, she would have loved to have waltzed with him at the ball!

The last few days had been awful. It was exhausting trying to pretend that everything was fine, reminding herself again and again that she'd done the right thing in turning down the chance to spend this last week with him. She had told Max that she wanted him to be happy, and she *did*. She'd just been unprepared for how much it would hurt when he took her advice and contacted Emma. Max was being a bit cagey about things and Allegra supposed it was none of her business, but she knew that he and Emma had met and that they were 'talking'. If she were Emma she would be moving heaven and earth to get back together with Max.

If she were Emma, she would never have left him in the first place.

Allegra had tried hard. She had thrown herself into work and been to every party she could blag herself into. She'd called William and invited him tonight, hoping that Max would somehow be less appealing in contrast, but instead the contrast had worked in Max's favour, and William was dazzled by Darcy. For all his intellect and ambition, he was clearly just as susceptible to Darcy's gorgeous face and even more gorgeous body as the next man, and Allegra herself might just as well have been invisible for all the notice he took of her.

It was lucky that she wasn't in love with William, Allegra reflected glumly. Nobody wanted her at the moment.

Max had wanted her. For a moment Allegra let herself remember the heat that had burned like wildfire along her veins, the taste of his skin and the wicked, wonderful torment of his mouth. The way the world had swung giddily around, the shattering pleasure. She could have had that again, but she had said no, and now it seemed that he was getting back together with Emma.

Allegra sighed. It made it so much worse when the only person you could blame for your misery was yourself.

CHAPTER NINE

THINK ABOUT YOUR career, Allegra told herself fiercely.
*Think about this amazing article you're going to write
that's going to impress the notoriously unimpressable
Stella and open doors for a career in serious journalism. Think about how pleased Flick is going to be with
you when your analysis of the latest political crisis hits
the headlines.*

But before she could tackle politics and the global economy she had to make a success of *Making Mr Perfect*.

Rousing herself, Allegra poked Max in the ribs as
William headed into the next room of the gallery, Darcy
breathlessly in tow. Caught up in the crowd, Allegra and
Max were trailing behind them.

'You're supposed to be impressing Darcy with your
knowledge of modern art,' she muttered.

'I would if there was any art here,' said Max. 'How does
this guy get away with it?' He studied a plate, encrusted
with dried baked beans, that was set carefully on a table
next to a rusty oil can. Craning his neck, he read the price
on the label and shook his head. 'He's having a laugh!'

'Digby Fox likes to challenge conventional expectations
about art,' Allegra said dutifully, but her heart wasn't in it.

'You can't tell me you actually like this stuff?'

'Not really,' she admitted, lowering her voice as if confessing to something shameful. 'I prefer paintings.'

Ahead of them, William had stopped in front of a collection of torn bin bags that were piled up against the stark gallery wall. 'A searing commentary on modern consumption,' he was saying as Max and Allegra came up.

Allegra was sure she heard Max mutter, 'Tosser.'

'One can't fail to be struck by the nihilistic quality of Digby's representation of quotidian urban life,' William went on while Darcy looked at him with stars in her eyes.

'It's powerful stuff,' she said, her expression solemn. 'It makes you feel *small*, doesn't it?'

William nodded thoughtfully, as if she had said something profound, and turned to Max, evidently deciding it was time to include him in the conversation. 'What do you think, Max?'

Max pretended to contemplate the installation. 'I think it's a load of old rubbish,' he pronounced at last.

William looked disapproving and Darcy disappointed, but a giggle escaped Allegra. Oh dear, sniggering at childish jokes didn't bode well for her future as a journalist with gravitas.

'Yes, well, shall we move on?' said William, taking Darcy's arm to steer her on to the next exhibit.

Max caught Allegra's eye. 'Let's get out of here,' he said. 'This is all such bollocks and we can't even get a decent drink.'

She opened her mouth to insist that they stayed, to point out that she had a job to do, but somehow the words wouldn't come. 'I don't suppose it would matter if we slipped out,' she said instead, looking longingly at the exit. Max was right. What was the point of staying? 'I'd better go and tell Darcy and William, though.'

'You really think they're going to notice that we've gone?'

'Probably not—' she sighed '—but allegedly Darcy's here for the article, and I invited William. I can't just abandon them without a word. I'll go and tell them I've got a headache and see you outside.'

It was amazing how her spirits lightened at the prospect of escaping with Max. By the time Allegra had pushed her way through the crush to William and Darcy, who were at the very back of the gallery by then, and then to the front again, she was hot and bothered and practically fell out of the door to find Max waiting for her.

Outside, a fine London mizzle was falling and Max's hair was already damp, but it was blessedly cool and Allegra fanned herself with the exhibition catalogue. 'That's better,' she said in relief, heading away from the noise of the gallery.

'I was beginning to think you'd changed your mind,' said Max, falling into step beside her.

'No way. I had to fight my way out, though. I can't believe how many people there were in there.'

Max snorted. 'Talk about the emperor's new clothes!'

'It was a bit rubbish,' Allegra allowed.

'Literally,' he said sardonically. 'So, do I gather Darcy wasn't devastated about me leaving her with William?'

'I'm afraid she was delighted. She might have thought you were pretty cute once, but she's forgotten all about you now that she's met William.'

'She wasn't really interested in me anyway,' said Max. 'She was just bored and looking for someone different.'

'Well, William's certainly that. Political aide and lingerie model…it's not an obvious combination, is it? But Darcy thinks William's really clever, and she loves the way he talks to her as if she'll understand what he says.'

A grunt. 'He was showing off, if you ask me.'

'Yes, but can you blame him? Darcy's so beautiful.'

'I can blame him for ignoring *you*,' said Max, scowling. 'I thought you two were going out?'

'Not really. We'd just had a drink a couple of times. It's not as if we'd ever—' Allegra stopped.

Slept together. Like she and Max had done.

There was a tiny pause while her unspoken words jangled in the silence. Allegra developed a sudden fascination with the shop window they were passing.

Max cleared his throat. 'Do you mind?' he asked. 'About William?'

'No, not really,' she said with a sigh. 'He's nice, but I don't think he's my kind of guy.'

'Who is?'

You are. The words rang so loudly in Allegra's head that for one horrified moment she thought that she had spoken them aloud.

'Oh, you know, the usual: tall, dark, handsome, filthy-rich...' She hoped he realised that she was joking. 'The truth is, I'm still trying to find a man who can match up to my Regency duke.'

'The terrace ravisher?'

'That's the one. I don't know anyone with a fraction of his romance,' she told Max.

'You don't think holding out for an aristocrat who's been dead for a couple of hundred years is going to limit your options a bit?'

'I'm hoping they'll invent a time travel machine soon,' said Allegra. 'In the meantime, I've got my fantasy to keep me warm.'

Max raised his brows. 'Whatever turns you on,' he said and they promptly plunged into another pool of silence.

He had turned her on. Allegra's pulse kicked as she remembered that night: the way they had grabbed each other, the frenzy of lust and heat and throbbing need. It hadn't been tender and beautiful. It had been wild and frantic and deliciously dirty. A flush warmed her cheeks, thinking about the things Max had done, the things she had done to him. She had turned him on too.

They had turned each other on.

Desperately trying to shove the memories away, Allegra was glad of Max's silence as they walked. At that time of the evening the back streets of Knightsbridge were quiet, apart from an occasional taxi passing, engine ticking and tyres shushing on the wet tarmac. Allegra was glad she had worn her boots rather than the more glamorous stilettos she'd dithered over. At least her boots were comfortable—well, relatively. She had to be careful not to twist her ankle falling off their substantial platform soles but otherwise they were almost as good as the trainers Max had once suggested she wear to work.

Max. Why did everything come back to him now?

She was agonizingly conscious of him walking beside her. His shoulders were slightly hunched and he had jammed his hands into his trouser pockets. Damp spangled his hair whenever he passed under a street lamp. He seemed distracted and she wondered if he was thinking about Shofrar. This time next week he'd be gone.

Something like panic skittered through Allegra at the thought, and she shivered involuntarily.

'You cold?' Max glanced at her.

'No, not really.'

His brows drew together as he studied her skimpy jacket. 'That's not enough to keep you warm. Didn't you bring a coat?'

'No, I—' But Max was already pulling off his jacket

and dropping it over her shoulders. It was warm from his body and the weight was incredibly reassuring.

'I'm not cold,' he said, 'and, besides, it doesn't matter if this shirt gets ruined. I am never, ever going to wear it again!'

'To be honest, I wouldn't have said it was really you,' said Allegra as she settled the jacket more comfortably around her, and Max smiled faintly.

'Don't tell Dickie that. It'll break his heart.'

She longed to take his arm and lean into his side, but she couldn't do that. Allegra kept her eyes on the pavement instead and clutched the two sides of the jacket together. She needed to show Max that she was fine about him leaving, that she had put that night they had shared behind her, just as she had said she would.

He had been in touch with Emma and it was too late now to tell him that she had changed her mind. It would make things even more awkward if he knew that she thought about him constantly, and that a dull ache throbbed in her chest whenever she thought about saying goodbye.

So she lifted her chin and summoned a bright smile. 'I don't suppose you'll have much need of a fancy wardrobe in Shofrar,' she said, determinedly cheerful.

'Nope. White short-sleeved shirt, shorts, long trousers for business meetings, and that's about it,' said Max. 'I won't ever need to dither over my wardrobe again.'

Allegra's smile twisted painfully. 'A life away from fashion. That'll make you happy.'

'Yes,' said Max, but he didn't sound as sure as he should have done. Of course he would be happy when he was there, he reassured himself. He couldn't wait. No styling sessions. No dancing lessons. No being told to roll up his cuffs, no need to consider what to wear. No messy house.

No Allegra.

The thought was a cold poker, jabbing into his lungs and stopping his breath. It was all for the best, of course it was, Max reminded himself with a shade of desperation. Going out to Shofrar was the next step in his career. It was what he had worked for, what he wanted. He would love it when he was there.

But he was going to miss her, there was no use denying it.

They were making their way slowly towards Sloane Street, along a side street clustered with antique shops and art galleries. Many were open still to cater for the after work crowd, and they had passed more than one gallery having a preview party much like the one they had just come from.

Allegra was absorbed in thought, her gaze on the window displays, which meant Max could watch her profile. Knowing that he could only look at her when she wasn't looking at him now made his chest tighten. When had she become so beautiful to him? Max's eyes rested hungrily on the curve of her cheek, on the clean line of her jaw and the lovely sweep of her throat. With her face averted he couldn't see her mouth, but he knew exactly how luscious it was, how her lips tipped upright at the corners and curved into a smile that lit her entire face.

God, he was going to miss her.

'Oh…' Unaware of his gaze, Allegra had stopped short, her attention caught by a single painting displayed in a gallery window.

The painting was quite small and very simple. It showed a woman holding a bowl, that was all, but something about the colours and the shapes made the picture leap into life. Compared to this, Digby Fox's installations seemed even more tawdry. This quiet painting was clearly special even though Max didn't have the words to explain how or why that should be so.

Holding the jacket together, Allegra was leaning forward to read the label. 'I thought so,' she said. 'It's a Jago Forrest. I've always loved his paintings.'

Max came closer to read the label over her shoulder. At least, he meant to read it, but he was too distracted by Allegra's perfume to focus. 'I've never heard of Jago Forrest,' he said.

'I don't think many people have. My art teacher at school was a fan, or I wouldn't have known about him either. He's famously reclusive, apparently... Oh, it looks like he died last year,' she went on, reading the label. Cupping her hands around her face, she peered through the window into the gallery. 'It says this is a retrospective exhibition of his works.'

'Why don't we go in and have a look?' said Max on an impulse. If you'd asked him a day earlier if he'd voluntarily go into an art gallery, he'd have scoffed, but the little picture in the window seemed to be beckoning him inside. 'At least we can look at some real art this evening as opposed to piles of rubbish.'

Inside, it was quiet and calm with none of the aggressive trendiness of the earlier gallery. A strikingly beautiful woman with cascading red curls welcomed them in and told them they were welcome to wander around, but she looked at Allegra so intently that Allegra clearly began to feel uncomfortable.

'If you're about to close...'

'No, it's all right. I'm sorry, I was staring at you,' said the woman. She had a faint accent that Max couldn't place. Eastern European, perhaps. 'We haven't met before, have we?'

'I'm sure I'd remember,' said Allegra. 'You've got such gorgeous hair.'

'Thank you.' The woman touched it a little self-consciously. 'I think perhaps I'm too old for such long hair now but Jago would never let me cut it.'

Her name, it turned out, was Bronya, and she had been Jago Forrest's muse for nearly twenty years, living with him in secluded splendour in an isolated part of Spain. She told Allegra that Jago had refused to see anyone, but that after he'd died she had decided to make his work accessible once more.

'But his portraits are so tender,' said Allegra. 'It's hard to believe that he disliked people that much.'

Bronya smiled faintly. 'He was a complicated man,' she said. 'Not always easy to live with, but a genius.' She looked sad for a moment. 'But I mustn't hold you up. Take your time looking round,' she said, gesturing them into the gallery. 'This is his most recent work down here, but some of his earlier paintings are upstairs if you'd be interested to see those too. Are you *sure* we've never met?' she said again to Allegra. 'You seem so familiar...'

Max found Jago Forrest's paintings oddly moving. Many were of Bronya, but he'd also painted countrywomen with seamed faces and gnarled fingers, and there were several young models he'd painted in the nude, portraying their bodies with such sensuousness that Max shifted uneasily.

'Let's go and look upstairs,' said Allegra eventually, and Max followed her up the spiral staircase. At the top she stopped so abruptly that he ran into her.

'Careful—' he began, but then he saw what had brought her up short. A huge portrait dominated the wall facing the staircase. It showed a young woman in a languorous pose, her arm thrown above her head and a satiated smile on her face. But it wasn't the overtly sexual feel to the painting that made Max's face burn. It was the woman's face, and the expression that was carnal and tender at the same time.

'She's beautiful, isn't she?' Bronya had followed them upstairs and stood beside them, misinterpreting their silence. She glanced at Max and Allegra. 'She and Jago had a passionate affair, oh, it must be twenty-five years ago now.'

She laughed lightly. 'I was jealous of her for a long time. I was so afraid that Jago would go back to her, but their affair must have ended very bitterly, I think. She was his passion, and I was his love, that's what he always told me. It's sad it didn't work out. You can see how much she loved him in her face, can't you?'

'Yes,' said Allegra in a strange wooden voice. She was very white about the mouth, and Max moved closer to put a steadying hand on her shoulder.

'Perhaps you recognise her?' Bronya paused delicately, looking curiously at Allegra.

'Oh, yes,' Allegra said, and turned to look straight at her. 'That's my mother.'

'Oh my God...' Bronya's hand crept to her mouth. 'Your eyes! That's why you seemed familiar...you've got Jago's eyes!' She stared at Allegra. 'You're his daughter!'

Max was worried about Allegra. She looked cold and lost as she stood on the pavement outside the gallery. He'd tried to put his arms round her, but she side-stepped his hug, holding herself together with an effort that left her rigid.

'I'll take you home,' he said, but she shook her head.

'I need to talk to my mother,' she said, and Max flagged down a taxi without arguing.

She hadn't said anything in the taxi, and now the taxi was pulling up outside Flick's house. 'Would you like me to come in with you?' he asked, not liking the frozen expression on her face.

'I'll be fine,' she said. 'I think this is a conversation Flick and I have to have on our own.'

'I'll wait then,' said Max.

'Don't be silly.' At least he'd brought a flicker of animation to her face and she even managed a smile of sorts. 'I could be hours. You go on home.'

Max didn't like it, but he could hardly insist on barging in with her so he waited until Allegra was inside before giving the taxi driver directions back to the house.

He couldn't settle. He threw himself on the sofa, then got up to go to the kitchen. He switched on the television, turned it off. He kept thinking of Allegra, and how she must have felt learning who her father was after all those years of not knowing. Why hadn't Flick told her? Max knew how much Allegra had yearned for a father. He'd seen how wistfully she had watched his father with Libby and, although his father treated her as an honorary daughter, it wasn't the same as having a father of her own.

The sound of her key in the lock had him leaping to his feet and he made it into the narrow hallway in time to see Allegra closing the front door. She was still wearing his jacket and when she turned her face wore an expression that made Max's heart turn over.

He didn't think. He just opened his arms and she walked right into them without a word.

Max folded her against him and rested his cheek on her hair as she clung to him, trembling. She was cold and tired and distressed, but holding her gave him the first peace he'd had in days.

'Come on,' he said gently at last. 'I'll get you a drink. You look like you need it.'

He made her sit on the sofa while he poured her a shot of whisky. Allegra eyed the glass he handed her dubiously. 'I don't really like whisky,' she said.

'Drink it anyway,' said Max.

Reluctantly she took a sip and choked but, after patting her chest and grimacing hugely, the colour started to come back to her cheeks and she tried again.

Max sat on the sofa beside her, but not too close. 'Better?'

'Funnily enough, yes.' She swirled the whisky around in the glass and her smile faded. 'I just made my mother cry,' she told Max. 'I don't feel very good about it.'

The indomitable Flick Fielding had *cried*? Max couldn't imagine it at all.

'What did she say when you told her about the portrait?'

'She was furious at first,' said Allegra. 'The portrait was supposed to have been destroyed, Bronya had no right to bring it to London, she would slap an injunction on her to make her remove it... She was pacing around her study, absolutely wild, but when I said it was a beautiful picture she just stopped and covered her face with her hands. It was like she just collapsed.' Allegra took another slug of whisky. 'I've never seen Flick cry before. It was awful.'

'Is it true? Was Jago Forrest your father?'

She nodded. 'Everything Bronya told us was true. They did have this incredibly passionate affair. Flick said that she was too young to know better but it's obvious even now that she loved him. Maybe she still does. She said that it almost destroyed her when he left her.'

Absently, Allegra sipped her whisky. 'It's funny to think of her being young and desperately in love, but it also makes a kind of sense now. She's hidden behind a mask of cool intelligence so that no one guesses that she was ever that vulnerable. I suppose keeping everyone at arm's length means that nobody has a chance to hurt you.' Allegra's expression was sad. 'Poor Flick.'

'Poor you,' said Max, unable to resist reaching over to tuck a stray hair back behind her ear. 'What happened?'

'Flick got pregnant but Jago didn't want a child.' Max could tell Allegra was struggling to keep her voice level, and he moved closer to put a comforting arm around her shoulders. She leaned into him gratefully, still cradling the glass between her hands.

'He gave her the money for a termination, but at the last moment, Flick decided she didn't want to go through with it and Jago was furious. He told her it was him or the baby, and she chose to have the baby.' Allegra swallowed. 'She was convinced that he loved her too much to really let her go, and she thought if she could just show him his child he'd change his mind.'

'And he didn't?'

Allegra shook her head. 'Flick said she took me round to his studio after I was born. She said she couldn't believe he would be able to resist me. She said I was perfect.' Her voice wobbled a little and she took another slug of whisky to steady it.

'She said, "You were absolutely perfect, and he looked at you as if you were a slug", and then he told her she would have to choose once and for all. He wanted her to get rid of me, apparently, and when she refused, that was it. He said that as far as he was concerned he'd washed his hands of the problem when he gave her money for the abortion, so she could forget asking him for any support.'

Max tightened his arm around Allegra. She was doing pretty well telling the story, but he'd seen her face when she repeated what Flick had told her about Jago's reaction. Doubtless it had been hard for Flick, but couldn't she have spared Allegra knowing that her father had looked at her as if she were a slug?

'And was that it?' he asked.

'She never saw him again and she was too angry and bitter to pursue him for support. She wouldn't discuss him at all.'

'I can see it was hard for her,' said Max, 'but why didn't she tell you? You had a right to know who your father was.'

Allegra let out a long sigh. 'She said she knew that if she told me I'd want to get in touch with Jago, and she was afraid that he'd reject me the way he'd rejected her. And I think, from what Bronya told us, he probably would have done. He was a genius, but he doesn't sound a very kind person. Flick said she couldn't bear the thought of him hurting me.' She swallowed hard. 'She said she was sorry—I don't think she's ever said that to me before. I hated seeing her so upset. It was like the world turning upside down.'

'You're upset too,' Max pointed out. 'It's been just as hard for you.'

'Well, at least I know who my father was now,' said Allegra bravely. 'And I understand Flick better. I used to think that she didn't really want me,' she confided, 'but she gave up her great passion for me, and she tried to protect me, so that feels good to know.'

'It was a lot for you to learn in one day,' said Max, a faint frown in his eyes. Allegra's composure was brittle and he could feel the tension in her body. 'How do you feel?'

'I'm fine,' she said brightly. 'I just…well, it's not every day you find out your father is a famous artist.'

'Would you rather not have known?' Max asked gently.

'No, it's better to know,' said Allegra. 'At least I can stop dreaming.' She smiled as if it hurt. 'I used to think that the only reason I didn't have a father was because Flick hadn't told him about me. I dreamt that he'd find out about me somehow and come and find me, and I'd be so precious to him. He'd look at me the way your dad looks at Libby.'

Her mouth started to wobble and she took her bottom lip between her teeth to keep it steady. 'So I suppose…I always, always wanted a father, but now it turns out that I had a father but he didn't want me.'

Her face crumpled and Max, who was normally terrified of tears, gathered her on to his lap as she let go of the storm of emotion at last. His throat tight, he held her softly and let her cry it all out until the wrenching sobs subsided to juddering sighs.

'Jago might have been a genius, but he was a fool,' he murmured, touching his lips to her hair without thinking. 'He missed out on knowing just what an amazing daughter he had.'

'I'm not amazing,' she said, muffled in his collar. 'My father was a genius, and Flick's got drive and intelligence, and I'm just…me. I'm not particularly good at anything.' Her voice clogged with tears again. 'And now I know what Flick gave up for me, I can understand just what a disappointment I am to her. I can't be what she wants me to be.'

'Then be what *you* want to be,' said Max. He put her away from him and held her at arm's length so that he could smooth her tangled hair back from her face and look straight into her eyes. 'You've spent your whole life trying to please your mother, Legs, and now it's time to please yourself. Decide what you want to do, and do it.'

Decide what you want. What Allegra really wanted was for Max not to go to Shofrar, but how could she beg him to stay when she knew how much the job meant to him? He'd let her cry over him, and she knew how much he must have hated that. Telling him how much she dreaded him going would have been little more than emotional blackmail.

So she'd knuckled the mascara from under her eyes and put on a smile and pretended that she was fine.

And now he was leaving. His bags were packed and sitting neatly in the hallway. The taxi to take him to Heathrow was due any minute.

The last few days had been a blur. Max's colleagues had thrown a leaving party for him. Allegra hadn't asked, but she was sure that Emma would have been there. The following night Dickie had insisted on farewell drinks in the pub Max had introduced him to. Darcy had come with William. She'd hugged Max and wished him well but it was obvious that she only had eyes for William now. Libby rang from Paris, Max's parents from Northumberland.

But now everybody had gone, the phone was silent and it was just the two of them waiting for the taxi in the sitting room. Allegra's heart was knocking painfully against her ribs. She didn't know whether she was dreading the moment of saying goodbye or longed for it to come so that at least this awful waiting would be over. It was early, not yet seven, and Allegra would normally have been in bed, but she couldn't let him leave without saying goodbye.

Without saying thank you.

She had come downstairs in her old pyjama bottoms and a camisole top, pulling on a cardigan against the crispness of the autumn morning. Her face was bare, her hair tousled.

There was too much to say, and not enough. Allegra's throat ached with the longing to tell Max that she loved him, but what would be the point? She didn't want to embarrass him, and besides, Emma would be waiting for him at the airport.

'Can you let me have Max's flight details?' Emma had rung the night before. Allegra had forgotten how friendly and downright *nice* Emma was. It was obvious that Max hadn't told her about the night he and Allegra had spent together, and it had certainly never crossed Emma's mind that Allegra might be any kind of rival.

Because she wasn't. She was the one who had told Max that they should pretend that night had never happened, Allegra reminded herself. She could hardly blame him when that was exactly what he did. It wasn't his fault that she had fallen in love with him.

Allegra was doing her best to convince herself that her feelings for him were just a temporary infatuation. Falling properly in love with him would be such a totally stupid thing to do. Again and again, Allegra ticked her way through a mental list of reasons why loving Max was a bad idea, and Emma was right there at the top.

Emma would be waiting for him when he got to the airport, and Allegra was fairly certain that she was going to tell Max that she loved him. If Allegra told him the same thing, it would put Max in an impossible situation.

Or maybe not. If you were Max, going out to work in the desert, and you had to choose between a ditzy fashionista and a genuinely nice, attractive fellow engineer who would be able to share your life completely, how hard a choice would it be?

Not very hard at all.

So Allegra stuck with agonising small talk when all she wanted to say was *I love you, I love you, I love you.*

Max was no more at ease and their conversation kept coming out in sticky dollops, only to dry up just when they thought they'd got going.

He hadn't learnt a thing about style. He was wearing one of his old suits, and if he hadn't deliberately chosen his dreariest shirt and tie it had been a lucky accident that he'd succeeded in putting on both. He looked dull and conventional.

He looked wonderful.

Allegra had to hug her arms together to stop herself reaching for him.

For the umpteenth time, Max pulled up his cuff to check his watch, but when his phone rang they both jumped.

'Taxi's here,' he said unnecessarily.

'Yes.' Allegra's throat had closed so tight it was all she could force out.

'So…it looks like this is it.'

'Yes.'

'I'd better go.'

Allegra was gripped by panic. She hadn't said anything that she wanted to! Why had she wasted these last precious minutes? Now all she could do was follow him out to the narrow hallway. She opened the door while Max picked up his briefcase and suitcase. He stepped out and looked at the taxi which was double-parked in the street before turning back to Allegra. He put down his cases again.

'Come out to the airport with me,' he said impulsively, and Allegra's heart contracted. She would have given anything to have an extra half hour with him in the taxi but she thought about Emma, waiting there to surprise him. It would spoil everything if she turned up too.

Emma was perfect for Max. He would realise that when he was in Shofrar, and he so deserved to be happy.

'I can't.' Allegra swallowed painfully. 'I need to get to work, but have a good flight,' she said with a wobbly smile, and stepped forward to give him what was meant to be a quick hug. 'I'll miss you,' she whispered.

Max's arms closed around her and he held her to him, so tightly that Allegra could hardly breathe, but she didn't care. She wanted to stay like that for ever, pressed against him, smelling him, loving him.

'I'll miss you too,' he whispered back.

They stood there, holding each other, neither wanting to be the first to let go, but eventually the taxi driver wound down his window. 'You planning on catching that plane, mate?' he called.

Reluctantly, Max released Allegra. 'I need to go.'

She nodded, tears shimmering in her eyes, and wrapped her arms around herself as she stood on the doorstep, careless of the cold on her bare feet, and watched as Max threw his cases into the back of the taxi. With his hand on the open door, he hesitated and looked back at Allegra as if he would say something else. For one glorious moment she thought that he was going to change his mind and stay after all, but in the end he just lifted his hand, got into the back of the taxi and shut the door.

The driver said something over his shoulder and put the taxi into gear. He put the indicator on and waited for a car that was coming up the street to pass. The car paused and flashed its lights politely to let him out. *No!* Allegra wanted to scream at it. *No, don't let him go!*

But it was too late. One last glimpse of Max through the window, and then the taxi was drawing away. Her heart tore, a slow, cruel rip as she watched it down the street, watched it turn left and out of sight.

And then he was gone.

CHAPTER TEN

'WHAT'S THE LATEST on the *Making Mr Perfect* piece?' Stella's steely gaze swept round the editorial conference before homing in on Allegra, who was doing her best to hide in the corner.

'Er, it's almost done,' said Allegra. The truth was that she couldn't bring herself to reread what she'd written about Max. It was all too raw.

She missed him terribly. In the past, when a relationship had ended, she'd been miserable for a day or two, but all it had taken was a new pair of shoes or a funny tweet to perk her up again. Now, it felt as if there was a jagged rip right through her heart, a bloody wound clawed open afresh every time she thought about Max. Missing him wasn't the vague sense of disappointment she'd felt before. It was the leadenness that had settled like a boulder in the pit of her stomach. It was the ache in her bones and the awful emptiness inside her.

Allegra was wretched. She hated going back to the house, hated going into the sitting room and seeing the empty sofa. She ached for the sight of him stretched out on it, rolling his eyes at her shoes. She missed the way he tsked at her untidy ways, the way that smile lurked at the corner of his mouth.

Without realising it, she had memorised every angle of

his face, every crease at the edges of his eyes. She could sketch him perfectly, but you couldn't hold a drawing, you couldn't touch it and feel it. You couldn't lean into it and make the world go away.

She hadn't been able to face finishing the article and had spent her time reading obsessively instead, escaping into the ordered world of her favourite Regency romances. A world where there were no exasperated civil engineers, no stupid jobs that took the hero overseas, no heartbreak that couldn't be resolved and sealed with a waltz around a glittering ballroom.

Now, with Stella's beady eye on her, Allegra struggled to remember that she had a job to do. 'I just need to tidy it up.'

'Done?' Stella snapped. 'How can it be done? You haven't been to the costume ball yet.'

Allegra cleared her throat. 'Unfortunately, we're going to have to miss out the ball. Max can't take part any longer. He's gone overseas.'

'What do you mean, *he's gone*?' Stella demanded. 'What about the article?'

'I thought I could end it at the Digby Fox preview.'

That didn't go down well. Stella's eyes bored into her. 'The whole point was to end with the ball,' she said icily. 'The fairy tale/knightly quest angle only makes sense if you follow it through to the ball. Get whatever-his-name-is to come back.'

Her immaculately polished fingernails drummed on the table while the rest of the editorial staff studiously avoided looking at either her or Allegra. Stella's displeasure could be a terrible thing to behold and nobody wanted to be associated with Allegra if she was in the firing line.

'I can't do that,' Allegra protested. 'He's got a job to do.'

Around the table there was a collective sucking in of breath. When Stella told you to do something, you did it. You didn't tell her that you couldn't. Not if you wanted to keep your job, anyway.

Incredibly, Stella didn't erupt. Her nails continued to click on the table, but her eyes narrowed thoughtfully. 'Then I suggest you find some way of including the ball anyway. Get Darcy to go with this new man of hers. She's always tweeting about how perfect he is. You could compare and contrast,' said Stella, warming to the idea. 'Show how what's-his-name was a failure and the new guy isn't.'

'His name's Max,' said Allegra clearly, ignoring the winces around her. 'And he isn't a failure!'

'He is as far as *Glitz* is concerned,' said Stella. 'Set up the ball and take a photographer. At least this way you can salvage something from the mess this article seems to have become.' Her eyes rested on Allegra's outfit. 'And sharpen yourself up if you want to stay at *Glitz*,' she added. 'You've let yourself go lately, Allegra. Those accessories are all wrong with that dress, and your shoes are so last season. It gives a bad impression.'

Allegra didn't like it, but she knew Stella was right. She *had* let herself go. She'd been too miserable to care about what she wore, but misery wasn't getting her anywhere. Every day when she checked her email she let the mouse hover over the 'new message' icon and thought about sending Max a message. She could keep it light, just ask how he was getting on. Just to hear from him.

But what would be the point? She didn't want to hear that he was enjoying Shofrar or that he was perfectly happy without her. She didn't want to hear that he had taken her advice and made it up with Emma. And what else could he tell her? That he loved her and missed her as much as she loved and missed him? Allegra couldn't see Max sitting at his computer and writing anything like that, even if he felt it. It just wasn't his style.

Once or twice, she poured out her feelings in an email, but she always came to her senses before she clicked 'send' and deleted it all instead. Max would be appalled, and it wasn't fair to embarrass him like that.

No, it was time to accept that Max had gone and that he wasn't coming back, time to stop reading and start deciding what to do with her life.

Be what you *want to be*. Max's words ran round and round in her head. Somewhere between finding out who her father was and Max leaving, Allegra had lost her certainty. What if Max had been right all along and she didn't really want to be a journalist at all?

The assignments Stella gave her now seemed increasingly silly. Allegra wrote a piece comparing the staying power of various lipglosses, and another on whether your hairdresser knew more about you than your beauty therapist. One day she did nothing but follow celebrity tweets and write a round up of all the banal things they'd said.

When Stella told her to invent some reader 'confessions' about their kinkiest sex exploits, Allegra couldn't even enjoy herself. She even got to work at home so that she didn't have to worry about anyone looking over her shoulder and raising their eyebrows. Once she would have found it fun, and let her imagination run wild, but now all she could think of was that night with Max, when they hadn't needed handcuffs or beads or uniforms. They hadn't needed a chandelier to swing from. They'd just needed each other.

Her blood thumped and her bones melted at the mere memory of it.

Allegra dropped her head into her hand and rubbed her forehead. Max was right about this too. She couldn't persuade herself any longer that working for *Glitz* was a stepping-stone to a glittering career in serious journalism. The *Financial Times* seemed further off than ever.

And who was she trying to fool? She didn't have what it took to be a serious journalist. She didn't even *want* to be a serious journalist.

Now all she had to do was decide what she *did* want to be. Allegra pushed her laptop away and picked up a pencil. She always thought better when she drew.

Except when she drew Max, when she just missed him.

With an effort, Allegra pushed him from her mind and sketched a quick picture of Derek the Dog instead. She drew him with his head cocked, his expression alert. He looked ready and eager to go. Allegra wished she felt like that.

Smiling, she let her pen take Derek on an adventure involving a double-decker bus, a steam engine, a jumbo jet and an old tugboat, and so absorbed was she that she missed the couture debut of the funkiest new designer in town. Everyone at *Glitz* had been buzzing about it, and Allegra too had one of the hottest tickets in fashion history.

She looked at her watch. If she rushed, she might still be able to squeeze in at the back, but then she'd have to get changed out of her vegging wear and she just couldn't be bothered.

Allegra sat back, startled by what she had just thought. Couldn't be bothered for *the* collection of the year? She examined herself curiously. Could it be true? Had she really changed that much?

Yep, she decided, she really had. Now all she had to do was think up a convincing excuse for her absence when everyone asked the next day. It would need to be a *really* good reason. Being struck down by a deadly virus wouldn't cut it. Any fashionista worth her salt would drag herself out of hospital if she had a ticket.

Allegra scratched her head with her pencil. She would just have to tell them she had been abducted by aliens— Struck by a thought, she ripped off a clean sheet from her drawing pad. Maybe it was time Derek went into space…

'You look amazing, like a fairy tale princess,' Allegra told Darcy. It was the night of the ball and they were squeezed in at the mirror in the Ladies', along with all the other women who were checking their lipstick and adjusting the necklines of their ball gowns. None of them looked as stunning as Darcy, though.

'I *feel* like a princess!' Pleased, Darcy swung her full skirt. The eighteenth-century-style dress was silver, with a embroidered bodice and sleeves that ended in a froth of lace at her elbows, and the skirt was decorated with bows and ruffles. On anyone else it would have seemed ridiculous, but Darcy looked magical. 'I always wanted to wear a dress like this when I was a kid,' she confided.

What little girl hadn't? Allegra had to admit to some dress envy, even though she knew she would never have been able to wear anything that fussy. She herself was in a slinky off-the-shoulder number that Dickie had found in one of the closets at *Glitz* that morning. It was a gorgeous red and it flattered her slender figure, but Allegra was feeling too dismal to carry it off.

'Ah, bah!' Dickie had said when she tried to tell him that. 'Eez *parfaite* for you.'

Allegra protested that she was only there as an observer to watch Darcy and William so she didn't need a ball gown, but Dickie had thrown such a hissy fit about her ingratitude that in the end she had just taken it.

Not that it mattered *what* she was wearing. Next to

Darcy, nobody was going to notice her. At least she wouldn't have to watch Max dancing with her. Remembering how they had learnt to waltz together brought such a stab of longing that Allegra had to bite her lip until it passed. She had left her hair loose, the way Max liked it. Oh, God, she *had* to stop thinking about him…

'Hey, I hear you wrote a book, you clever thing,' said Darcy, leaning into the mirror and touching the tip of her ring finger to her flawless cheekbones, just to check that her make up was perfect. It was.

Allegra was startled out of her wretchedness. 'Who told you that?'

'William.' Darcy practically licked her lips every time she said his name. The two of them had been inseparable ever since the preview. It was an unlikely combination, the political aide and the lingerie model, but they were clearly mad about each other. 'Your mum told him. He says she's boasting about you to everyone.'

'*Really?*' Allegra was surprised. Flick had been delighted to hear that her daughter was planning to resign from *Glitz* as soon as the *Making Mr Perfect* article was finished, but she was much less impressed by Allegra's idea of working freelance until she could find a publisher for her Derek the Dog stories.

'An illustrator?' she had echoed in dismay, and then her mouth tightened. 'This is because of Jago, isn't it?'

'No,' said Allegra evenly, 'I'm never going to be an artist like him, just like I'm never going to be a journalist like you.' She thought about her old dreams. 'I'm not a princess in disguise or a governess in a Regency romance. I'm just ordinary, and I'm going to stop trying to be anything but myself. I draw silly little pictures of animals. It's not much, but it's what I can do.'

Flick had been taken aback at first. 'Well, I *suppose* I

could introduce you to some agents,' she had offered reluctantly at last.

'Thanks,' said Allegra, 'but I've already approached one. She likes my illustrations, but she's less keen on the story. She's talking about teaming me up with a writer she knows.'

'Oh.'

Allegra suspected Flick was rather miffed by the fact that she hadn't traded on her famous mother's connections, but if Flick had talked about her to William she must have come round. As far as Allegra knew, Flick had never once told anyone that she was working for *Glitz*. The fact that she might have done something to please her mother at last gave Allegra a warm feeling around her heart for the first time since Max had left.

William was waiting for them in the lobby of the hotel, carrying off his Prince Charming costume with aplomb. Remembering how seriously he had talked the first time she had met him, Allegra smiled to herself. He really must be smitten by Darcy if he was prepared to dress up. 'I'd rather stick pins in my eyes,' Max had said.

In contrast, Dom, the photographer, stood out from the crowd in his jeans and leather jacket. He took some photos of William and Darcy together and then they all moved into the ballroom, where the ball was already in full swing.

Allegra found a place on the edge of the room. It was a classic ballroom, with glittering chandeliers and a high, elaborately decorated ceiling. One wall was punctuated with elegant long windows, open in spite of the dreary November weather to let some much needed air into the crowded ballroom. An orchestra at one end was playing a vigorous waltz, and couples in gorgeous costumes whirled around the floor.

Everything was just as Allegra had always dreamed

a ball would be. It was perfect—or it would have been if
only Max had been there with her. The thought of him
triggered a wave of loneliness that hit her with such force
that she actually staggered. Her knees went weak and all
the colour and gaiety and movement of the scene blurred
before her eyes.

She couldn't bear it without Max.

Blindly, she started for the doors. It was noisy and
crowded and empty without him. She would wait for Dom
outside. It was too painful to be here, with the music and
the laughter and the memories of how she and Max had
waltzed around the sitting room, of how useless they had
both been, how they had laughed together.

'Excuse me…sorry…sorry…' Allegra squeezed her
way through the throng, too intent on escaping to enjoy
the fantastic costumes. She kept her head down so that
no one would see the tears pooling in her eyes and it was
perhaps inevitable that she ended up bumping into a solid
male body.

'Sorry…I'm so sorry…' Desperate to get away, she
barely took in more than an elaborate waistcoat. Another
Prince Charming in full eighteenth-century dress, she had
time to think before she side-stepped to pass him, only to
be stopped by a hand on her arm.

'Would you do me the honour of this dance?'

Allegra had already started to shake her head when
something familiar about the voice filtered through the
music and the chatter and her heart clenched. How cruel
that her longing should make it sound so like Max's.

Blinking back her tears, she summoned a polite smile
and lifted her eyes from the waistcoat and past the ex-
travagant cravat to Prince Charming's face underneath
his powdered wig.

'I'm afraid I'm just lea—' Her voice faded as her gaze

reached his eyes and she blinked, certain that she must be imagining things, but when she opened her eyes again he was still there.

'Max?' she quavered, still not sure that her longing hadn't conjured him up out of thin air.

'I know, I look a prat,' said Max.

Astonishment, joy, incredulity, shock: all jostled together in such a fierce rush that Allegra couldn't catch her breath. For a stunned moment all she could do was stare in disbelief. Max was out in the desert, in shorts and sunglasses, not dressed up as a fairy tale prince in a crowded ballroom.

'*Max?*'

'Yes, it's me.' Incredibly, he looked nervous.

'Wh…what are you doing here?' Still unable to believe that it could really be true, she had to raise her voice above the noise in the ballroom, and Max leant closer to make sure that she could hear.

'I've been doing some thinking, and I decided it would be a shame if we wasted all those waltzing lessons,' he told her, and he held out his hand. 'Shall we dance?'

In a blur, Allegra let him lead her onto the floor, finding a place on the edge of the other couples who were whirling around the floor in an intimidatingly professional fashion. She didn't understand anything, but if this was a dream, she didn't want to wake up.

Max swung her round into position. He held one of her hands in his, and set the other on his shoulder so that he could take hold of her waist. 'Okay,' he yelled, looking down at their feet. 'Remember the box? Let's go…*one*, two, three, *one*, two, three…'

They made a mess of it at first, of course. They stumbled and trod on each other's toes, but all at once, magically, they clicked and found the rhythm. True, they could only go round and round the 'box' but they were on the floor and they were moving together in time to the music—sort of. Allegra's heart was so full, she was crying and floating in delirious joy at the same time.

Laughing through her tears, she lifted her face to Max's. 'We're *waltzing!*' she shouted.

'Ready to try a new manoeuvre?' he shouted back and, without waiting for her answer, he lunged with her further into the crowd. This was a whole new step outside their safe box, as they had never really mastered turning, but Max had a determined look on his face and Allegra followed as best she could.

'Where are you going?' she yelled in his ear.

'Terrace,' he said briefly, face set as he concentrated on steering her through the throng of dancers.

The *terrace?* Allegra thought about the chill drizzle that was falling outside, but it was too noisy to have a conversation and, anyway, Max seemed set on the idea. He danced her grimly across the floor. They'd lost their rhythm again and kept bumping into other couples, but somehow they made it to the other side. Max took a deep breath and somehow manoeuvred them through one of the windows and out onto the terrace that overlooked the hotel's garden.

'That was harder than I thought,' he said, and let Allegra go.

Outside, the air was damp and cold, but it was blissfully quiet after the noise in the ballroom. Still gripped by a sense of unreality, Allegra shook her head slightly.

'Max, what are you doing here? I thought you were in Shofrar.'

'I was, but I told Bob that I needed to come back to London.'

She looked concerned. 'Aren't you enjoying the job?'

'The job's great.' It was. 'It's everything I ever wanted
to do, and the desert is beautiful. I wish you could see it,
Legs. The light is extraordinary.'

'Then why come back to London?' she asked, puzzled.

Max took a deep breath. 'Because you weren't there,'
he said. 'The thing is…' He'd rehearsed this speech in
his head but now that the moment had come, his mind
had gone blank. 'The thing is, I missed you,' he finished
simply.

'But…what about Emma?' Allegra's eyes were huge.
She looked as if she was unsure whether she was dreaming or not, and Max couldn't blame her. One minute she
had been heading out of the ballroom and the next she
was faced with an idiot in full eighteenth-century dress.

'She told me she wanted to say goodbye to you at the
airport,' Allegra went on. 'I thought she was going to suggest that you got back together.'

'She did,' said Max, remembering how long it had taken
him to understand what Emma was saying. Her timing
hadn't been good, to say the least. His mind had been too
full of Allegra, standing on the doorstep, watching as he
drove away. 'She said she wanted to try again, that she'd
realised that friendship was a better foundation for marriage than passion.'

'Which was what you'd said all along.'

'I did say that and I believed it, but I've changed my
mind,' Max said. 'Friendship isn't enough on its own, nor
is passion. You need both. I told Emma that I'd like to be
friends, but I knew that I'd never be happy unless I could
be with you.'

'With me…' she echoed incredulously, but a smile lit
her eyes, and he took hold of her hands.

'I love being with you, Legs. I don't care what we're
doing. Even when you were making me dress up and make

a fool of myself, it was fun. I missed being able to talk to you and hear you laugh, I missed you nagging about my clothes. God, I even found myself rolling my cuffs up!' he said, and Allegra laughed unsteadily.

Tears were trembling on the end of her lashes and Max tightened his grasp on her fingers, desperate to tell her how he felt before she cried. 'I missed you as more than a friend, though. I wanted to be able to touch you and feel you…I haven't been able to stop thinking about that night. It's never been like that for me before,' he said honestly. 'It was as if everything else had been a practice and suddenly with you it was the real thing. Like I'd never understood before that was how it was supposed to be. I can't explain it. With you, it just felt right…' He trailed off, seeing the tears spilling down her cheeks. 'Don't cry, Legs, please. I just wanted to tell you how I felt.'

'I'm crying because I'm happy,' she said, trying in vain to blink back the tears. 'Oh, Max, that was how it was for me too.'

The tight band around Max's chest unlocked and he released her hands to take her face between his palms.

'Allegra,' he said unevenly, 'I know I'm stuffy and I can't dance and I've got no dress sense but I love you. That's why I came back. I had to tell you.'

Incredibly, she was smiling still. 'I love you too,' she said, sliding her arms around his waist. 'I've missed you so much.'

A smile dawned in Max's eyes as his heart swelled. Tenderly, he grazed her jaw with his thumbs. 'You love me?' he repeated, dazed at the wonder of it.

'I do,' she said and her voice broke. 'Oh, Max, I do.' And she clung to him as he kissed her at last, the way he had dreamt of kissing her for so many long and lonely nights, so many bleak days.

She kissed him back, a long, sweet kiss edged with the same giddy relief at having been pulled back from an abyss at the last moment. They ran their hands hungrily over each other, a remembered inventory of pleasure. Heedless of the drizzle that was rapidly turning to rain, they forgot the ball, forgot the cold, forgot everything but the dazzling joy of being able to touch each other again, feel each other again.

Max was rucking up Allegra's skirt with an urgent hand before a splatter of rain right down his neck brought him reluctantly back to reality. Grumbling at the weather, he pulled Allegra into the shelter of an overhanging balcony and rested his forehead against hers.

'I wish you'd said something before you left,' she said, softening her criticism by clinging closer. 'I've been so wretched without you.'

'I couldn't. You made it pretty clear that night was just a one-off as far as you were concerned,' he pointed out. 'We've got different lives, you said, and you were right. I could see that. God, Legs, I only had to look at you. You were having so much fun in London. You've got a great life, doing what you want to do. You're so bright and warm and funny and gorgeous. How could I possibly imagine you wanting to be with a boring civil engineer?'

Allegra couldn't help laughing. 'Nobody looking at you dressed up as Prince Charming could possibly describe you as boring, Max!' For the first time she took in the full glory of his costume. His jacket was made of plum-coloured velvet, and he wore tight breeches and silk socks held up with garters. The satin waistcoat was the same colour as the jacket, and an intricately arranged necktie frothed at his throat. 'Where on earth did you find your outfit?'

'Dickie got it for me.'

'Dickie!' She gaped at him. 'He didn't tell me that you'd been in touch!'

'I asked him not to and, anyway,' said Max, drawing her back into him and putting on a superior air, 'I'm not Prince Charming, I'm a duke.'

'*Are* you?' Allegra tucked in the corners of her mouth to stop herself laughing.

He pretended to be hurt. 'I thought you'd have recognised a Regency duke when you saw one!'

'Hmm, I think you and Dickie might have slipped a century,' said Allegra. 'My Regency duke didn't wear a powdered wig.'

'Thank God for that!' Max snatched off his wig and cast it aside, before taking Allegra back in his arms. 'I couldn't find a time travel machine, so this was the closest I could get to your fantasy,' he confessed. 'I had this great plan. I was going to recreate it for you exactly,' he told her as her eyes widened. 'I was going to waltz you out onto the terrace, just the way you told me about, and then I was going to tell you how passionately I loved you and beg you to marry me, and bowl you over with the romance of it all. I wanted you to have the perfect proposal.'

'But I made a mess of it,' he said. 'The fact is, I'm not a duke, I can't dance, I look like an idiot and it's raining. Where's the romance in that?'

'It's the most romantic thing I could imagine,' said Allegra, her voice tight with emotion. 'The duke's just a fantasy, but you're *real*.' She kissed him softly. 'Maybe you can't dance, and no, you're not the sharpest dresser, but you're perfect for me and I love you just as you are.'

'What, even buttoned up to my collar?'

'Even then.'

Max grinned, pleased. 'Hey, you really must love me,' he said and she laughed.

'I really do,' she said, and he kissed her again, pressing her against the wall until they were both breathless and shaky with desire.

'We've wasted so much time,' Max grumbled against her throat. 'I wish I'd known how you felt before I left.'

'I couldn't tell you,' Allegra protested, snuggling closer. 'You told me yourself you needed someone sensible like Emma.'

'I thought that too,' he said, as his hands slid possessively over her curves. 'But it turns out that I need fun and frivolity instead. I've asked Bob if I can transfer back to the London office. I thought even if my Regency duke impersonation didn't work, it would be easier to be in the same city. At least then I'd get to see you.'

Allegra pressed closer, loving the hard demand of his hands. 'Ask him if you can stay in Shofrar after all,' she said. 'It turns out that I don't have any fun if I'm not with you, so why don't I come with you?'

'But what about your job at *Glitz*?'

'Well, I've made some decisions since you left.' She told him what the agent had said about her drawings. 'It's a long shot but who knows? It might come off and I can always try my hand at other illustrations. I'm sure I'll be able to keep myself busy during the day, anyway,' she said. 'And you can keep me busy at night,' she added with a wicked smile.

'I'll do my best.' Max kissed her again, and that was the last they spoke for some time. Careless of the rain puddling on the terrace around them, oblivious to the music spilling out from the ballroom, they lost themselves in the heady wonder of touch and taste.

'You know we'll have to get married?' said Max eventually, resting his cheek against her hair.

Allegra tipped back her head to smile at him. 'I'm counting on it,' she said.

Max felt his heart swell until it was jammed almost painfully against his ribs. 'Allegra...' he said, shaken by the rush of emotion. 'I don't want to be apart from you again. How soon do you think we can arrange a wedding?'

'As soon as possible.' Allegra looked demure. 'I'm sure Dickie will be happy to find a flowery waistcoat for you to wear.'

'I don't mind what I wear as long as you're standing there saying "I do",' he said.

'You might regret saying that!'

'The only thing I'll regret is not telling you I loved you earlier,' he said seriously, and her lips curved under his as he kissed her once more.

Inside, the orchestra struck up another waltz, and they smiled at each other as they moved into the dance. Max's arm was around her, his fingers warm and firm around hers as they danced through the puddles, heedless of the rain.

Allegra's heart was floating. 'This is perfect,' she said, as Max twirled her around. 'Waltzing on the terrace, a proposal of marriage... What more could I want?'

'I seem to remember something about being ravished against a balustrade,' said Max, and his eyes gleamed in the dim light as he danced her over to it. Turning so that she was pressed against the balustrade, he smiled lovingly down into her face. 'You, my darling, are about to have your dream come true.'

Allegra heaved a contented sigh and wound her arms around his neck to pull him closer. 'It already has,' she said.

MAKING MR PERFECT by Allegra Fielding
Can you create the perfect boyfriend? We set one
guy a modern-day quest, a series of challenges he

had to complete successfully in order to win the love of today's demanding damsels who want their man to be everything: socially skilled, emotionally intelligent, well-dressed, practical, artistic; a cook, a dancer, a handyman...

We took an uptight, conventionally dressed bloke with zero interest in the arts and a horror of the dance floor, and we asked him if he could change. Could he learn to dress stylishly and navigate a cocktail menu without cringing? Was he prepared to throw away the takeaway menu and go to the effort of cooking a meal from scratch? Could he talk knowledgeably about modern art? Could he learn how to waltz?

If you've been following Max's progress over the past few weeks, you'll know that he sailed through some of the 'tests' but crashed and burned on others, notably the exhibition of contemporary art installations. In spite of his grumbling, Max claims to have learnt something from the process. 'I learnt to make an effort,' he says. 'I learnt to think about what women really want and—more importantly, I gather—not to button my collar quite so tightly.'

But the truth is that Max didn't learn nearly as much as I did. Whether he succeeded or failed, he remained resolutely himself. Yes, he made an effort, but he didn't change. He's never going to be a snappy dresser. He's always going to prefer a beer to a fancy drink, and he's still going to have to be dragged kicking and screaming to anything remotely smacking of the arts. The tests were pointless: anyone can pretend, but what's the point of pretending? Nobody wants to fall in love with a fake.

There's no formula for a perfect man, unless it's for a man who doesn't need to pretend, a man who's happy to be himself. A man who might not be able to dance, but who makes you laugh and holds you when you cry, who makes you feel safe and gives you the strength to be the best you can be. Who will stay by your side, through good times and bad. A man who makes you feel the most beautiful and desirable woman in the world when he kisses you.

A man who sees you for what you really are, and who loves you anyway.

So let's not ask our men to be everything. Let's love them with all their imperfections, because those are what make them who they are. Max doesn't have a single one of the qualities I once thought necessary in my perfect man, and yet somehow that's exactly what he is: my very own Mr Perfect.

* * * * *

Mills & Boon® Hardback

January 2014

ROMANCE

MEDICAL

Mills & Boon® Large Print

January 2014

ROMANCE

Challenging Dante — Lynne Graham
Captivated by Her Innocence — Kim Lawrence
Lost to the Desert Warrior — Sarah Morgan
His Unexpected Legacy — Chantelle Shaw
Never Say No to a Caffarelli — Melanie Milburne
His Ring Is Not Enough — Maisey Yates
A Reputation to Uphold — Victoria Parker
Bound by a Baby — Kate Hardy
In the Line of Duty — Ami Weaver
Patchwork Family in the Outback — Soraya Lane
The Rebound Guy — Fiona Harper

HISTORICAL

Mistress at Midnight — Sophia James
The Runaway Countess — Amanda McCabe
In the Commodore's Hands — Mary Nichols
Promised to the Crusader — Anne Herries
Beauty and the Baron — Deborah Hale

MEDICAL

Dr Dark and Far-Too Delicious — Carol Marinelli
Secrets of a Career Girl — Carol Marinelli
The Gift of a Child — Sue MacKay
How to Resist a Heartbreaker — Louisa George
A Date with the Ice Princess — Kate Hardy
The Rebel Who Loved Her — Jennifer Taylor

Mills & Boon® Hardback
February 2014

ROMANCE

A Bargain with the Enemy	Carole Mortimer
A Secret Until Now	Kim Lawrence
Shamed in the Sands	Sharon Kendrick
Seduction Never Lies	Sara Craven
When Falcone's World Stops Turning	Abby Green
Securing the Greek's Legacy	Julia James
An Exquisite Challenge	Jennifer Hayward
A Debt Paid in Passion	Dani Collins
The Last Guy She Should Call	Joss Wood
No Time Like Mardi Gras	Kimberly Lang
Daring to Trust the Boss	Susan Meier
Rescued by the Millionaire	Cara Colter
Heiress on the Run	Sophie Pembroke
The Summer They Never Forgot	Kandy Shepherd
Trouble On Her Doorstep	Nina Harrington
Romance For Cynics	Nicola Marsh
Melting the Ice Queen's Heart	Amy Ruttan
Resisting Her Ex's Touch	Amber McKenzie

MEDICAL

Tempted by Dr Morales	Carol Marinelli
The Accidental Romeo	Carol Marinelli
The Honourable Army Doc	Emily Forbes
A Doctor to Remember	Joanna Neil

Mills & Boon® Large Print
February 2014

ROMANCE

HISTORICAL

MEDICAL